Donald MacKenzie and The Murder Room

>>> This title is part of The Murder Room, our series dedicated to making available out-of-print or hard-to-find titles by classic crime writers.

Crime fiction has always held up a mirror to society. The Victorians were fascinated by sensational murder and the emerging science of detection; now we are obsessed with the forensic detail of violent death. And no other genre has so captivated and enthralled readers.

Vast troves of classic crime writing have for a long time been unavailable to all but the most dedicated frequenters of second-hand bookshops. The advent of digital publishing means that we are now able to bring you the backlists of a huge range of titles by classic and contemporary crime writers, some of which have been out of print for decades.

From the genteel amateur private eyes of the Golden Age and the femmes fatales of pulp fiction, to the morally ambiguous hard-boiled detectives of mid twentieth-century America and their descendants who walk our twenty-first century streets, The Murder Room has it all. **>>>**

The Murder Room
Where Criminal Minds Meet

themurderroom.com

T0352484

Donald MacKenzie 1908–1994

Donald MacKenzie was born in Ontario, Canada, and educated in England, Canada and Switzerland. For twenty-five years MacKenzie lived by crime in many countries. 'I went to jail,' he wrote, 'if not with depressing regularity, too often for my liking.' His last sentences were five years in the United States and three years in England, running consecutively. He began writing and selling stories when in American jail. 'I try to do exactly as I like as often as possible and I don't think I'm either psychopathic, a wayward boy, a problem of our time, a charming rogue. Or ever was.'

He had a wife, Estrela, and a daughter, and they divided their time between England, Portugal, Spain and Austria.

Raven's Shadow

Donald MacKenzie

An Orion book

Copyright © The Estate of Donald MacKenzie 1984

The right of Donald MacKenzie to be identified as the author of this work has
been asserted in accordance with the Copyright, Designs and Patents Act 1988.

This edition published by
The Orion Publishing Group Ltd
Orion House
5 Upper St Martin's Lane
London WC2H 9EA

An Hachette UK company
A CIP catalogue record for this book is available from the British Library

ISBN 978 1 4719 0545 2

All characters and events in this publication are fictitious and any resemblance
to real people, living or dead, is purely coincidental.

No part of this publication may be reproduced, stored in a retrieval system or
transmitted in any form or by any means without the prior permission in writing
of the publisher, nor be otherwise circulated in any form of binding or cover
other than that in which it is published without a similar condition, including this
condition, being imposed on the subsequent purchaser.

www.orionbooks.co.uk

For Stephen and Michelle

Cooney

The man behind the wheel of the unmarked police
Jaguar had lank yellow hair like a surfer's, the amber
eyes of a hound and a thin-lipped face. The clothes he
was wearing were expensive; a Burberry trenchcoat,
blazer, grey flannel trousers and Piero de Monzi
loafers. His name was Detective Sergeant Cooney
and he was the youngest member of the Serious
Crimes Squad. The silencer screwed to the barrel of
the thirty-two calibre pistol in his pocket dug into his
ribs as he leaned towards his partner.

'What's the problem, Dave?'

The other man shook his head. 'Who said anything
about problems? I didn't even open my mouth.'

Cooney fixed him with a cool stare. 'A guy like you
doesn't have to speak to show what he's thinking.'

Detective Inspector Slade grunted. He was eighteen
years older than Cooney, a top heavy man with wispy
grey hair carefully arranged to conceal a bald patch.
His sparse moustache and eyebrows matched his hair
and there were broken veins in the side of his nose.
His suit was of nondescript cut and material while the
raincoat thrown across the back seat bore the signs of
canteen meals eaten at speed.

The Jaguar was parked close to the river in Putney.
It was early November and the light from the street

lamps shone on wet garden walls. The block of flats behind the walls was partially obscured by the trees. It was twenty past six by the clock on the dash. Cooney dug into his blazer and swallowed a couple of Diludin capsules.

Slade made a face. After twenty-five years in London he still had a West Country burr. 'Someone's going to catch you with that stuff on you one of these days. I don't know why the hell you do it.'

'My nerves need steadying,' said Cooney. 'We're in a high-risk business, Dave.'

'Bullshit!' said Slade.

'I tell you they're on prescription,' lied Cooney. He had been doing speed for nine months and enjoyed the rush that it gave him. His mind became honed to laser perception.

Slade pushed his gloved hands deeper into his jacket pockets, they were shaking.

'You're a crafty bugger, Cooney. All these months at it and I never caught on.'

Cooney smiled. 'I've been waiting for the big one, Dave. Saving it for you.'

'I should have been on the firm from the start,' argued Slade. 'I never did like mysteries. Even now I don't know the name of the geezer.'

'The less you know the better,' said Cooney. 'All you need in your head is the way we cut up. The man in Amsterdam gets ten per cent for his information. We split the rest down the middle and that's all there is to it. OK?'

'OK,' Slade said grudgingly. He worried his sparse moustache. 'I'll be honest with you, Terry. I don't like the idea of the shooter.'

Cooney leaned back in his seat, looking up at the car roof lining.

'Here we go again! Look, do you want to do it or not?'

'Of course I want to do it,' said Slade. 'But you know me and guns. The fucking things make me nervous!'

Cooney laid his hand on the other man's knee. 'Look, Dave. You're forty-six years old and you haven't a pot to piss in. Your marriage is a mess and you couldn't make superintendent if they blew the answers up your ass. I'm talking to you as a friend, Dave. I'm giving you the chance to get out of all that. Trust me!'

Slade removed the hand from his knee. 'You'll be the first to know when I don't, mate.'

Cooney switched on the dash light and looked at the clock again. It was half-past six. He turned off the light and pocketed the ignition keys.

'OK, let's go. Keep your hands in your pockets and let me do the talking.'

They walked down the empty street and crossed the car park at the rear of the flats. The wind had dropped and the river was covered with mist. They picked their way down a flight of steps, treading on piles of rain-sodden leaves. Cooney inserted a key in the fireproof door, letting them into a white-washed passageway lit by naked bulbs. The furnace room was silent except for the hum of the oil-fired burners. Wooden stairs rose to a baize-lined door that opened into a discreetly-lit corridor. The hush that greeted them belonged to a place of worship. Brass numerals glittered on dark varnished doors. The window embrasures were set with flowers. The two men were out of sight of the lobby. Thick carpeting absorbed the sound of their feet as they tiptoed past the lift to the staircase. The Diludin was into Cooney's bloodstream and he trod lightly. Slade's pace was laborious. Beads of sweat had formed on his forehead. The fourth floor was a replica of those below. Apartment L was protected by three locks, an Ingersol and two heavy duty mortise locks. An optic spyglass was set in the door at eye-level. Cooney pressed the bell and stepped back with Slade just behind him. A disembodied eye appeared at the spyhole. The door opened on a short length of chain. The willowy man behind it was of medium height and build with a pale face and hair as straight and black as a Chinaman's. He was wearing British Airways uniform trousers, white shirt and black tie. His eyes roved from Cooney to Slade.

'Who's this?' he asked flatly.

'The extra man,' said Cooney.

The pilot took a closer look at Slade who nodded greeting. He was still sweating profusely. The pilot was plainly unimpressed.

'Nobody's said anything to me about an extra man.'

Cooney shrugged indifferently. 'I only do what I'm told. Why don't you check? One thing's for sure. We can't stand out here all night.'

The chain rattled free and the pilot opened the door. A uniform tunic and raincoat hung on a stand in the hall. The pilot led them into a sitting-room furnished in blond oak, blue carpet and curtains and some pictures of seagulls. Open doors offered glimpses of bedroom, bathroom and kitchen. Slade stood near the window, an ingratiating smile on his face, his hands still deep in his pockets. The pilot's gaze followed him suspiciously.

'I've heard nothing about an extra man and you know what the rules are. Nobody comes here but you.'

The speed made Cooney see very clearly. Slade's mixture of uneasy confidence was patently false.

'Look,' said Cooney. 'I've got other things to do and I'm running late as it is. Call the boss if you're worried.'

Indecision clouded the pilot's face. 'I don't have the number.'

'I can give it to you,' said Cooney. He scribbled on a page in his notebook and gave it to the pilot.

The pilot spun the dial, his eyes still on Slade who was whistling soundlessly.

'No answer,' the pilot said after a while.

Cooney could have told him as much. The number was his own and he knew that his sister was out.

'Why don't you try again later?' he said.

The pilot's smile was disarming. 'I'm not trying to be difficult. It's just that rules are rules. Do you people want a drink before you move on? I'll get your stuff ready in the meantime.'

'It'll have to be a quick one,' said Cooney. He slipped on the chamois leather gloves as the pilot turned and then took two long steps forward. He jammed the silencer against the back of the pilot's head and pulled the trigger. The noise was no louder than that of a light bulb exploding. The pilot pitched forward as though caught by a tripwire. He fell face down, arms extended, kicked a few times, then was still. Splinters of bone gleamed among the brains and blood that oozed from the wound. Cooney bent swiftly and reclaimed his telephone number from the pilot's lifeless fingers. Slade's shocked face was watching every move from the window. He looked like a man grown ten years older, shrunken in his shabby suit. He opened his mouth a couple of times but no sound came forth.

Cooney knelt beside the pilot's body, feeling inside the collar. He yanked out a small key fastened on a slim gold chain. Then he straightened his back and opened the drinks cupboard. Lying on the bottom shelf was a small Belgian-made automatic.

'It was him or us, Dave,' he said, turning his head. 'The bastard was going to use it!'

Slade was still incapable of speech. His cheeks were the colour of putty. Cooney splashed Scotch into a glass and stuck it into his partner's gloved hand.

'Don't worry, Dave,' he said. 'Get this inside you. It'll be days before they find him.'

Slade swallowed unsteadily, staring down at the key that Cooney had given him.

'The safe's in the bedroom,' said Cooney. 'Get the gear and leave the key in the lock. I'm going to take a quick look outside.'

Slade hesitated, still stunned by the implications of what had just happened. 'Jesus Christ, Terry,' he said, shaking his head.

'Do it!' said Cooney.

Slade moved towards the bedroom like a sleep-walker. A flight-bag perched on a chair. The bag was open. Inside was a bottle of duty-free vodka. A Patek Philippe wristwatch lay on the bedside table. Lights came on inside as Slade opened the built-in ward-robe. White shirts were stacked on the shelves. Black shoes perched on rails under the nylon suit-hangers. Sweat soaked Slade's body. Every thought in his head related to danger. A man had just been murdered and he was part of it. He should have known better than to trust this crazy bastard. He bent his head and stepped into the cupboard. The panel that concealed the safe was half-open. He slid it back as far as it would go, revealing the Chubb Lombard Special cemented into the masonry. It was fire-proof and blast-proof, impervious to any assault short of removing half-a-ton of high-grade steel and reinforced brickwork.

He turned the key and the safe door swung out. There was nothing inside except for a small box heavily sealed with red wax. He left the key in the lock as instructed. Cooney came from the hall as Slade entered the sitting-room. Slade gave him the box.

'Wipe your face,' said Cooney. 'You're sweating like a pig.'

Slade used his dirty handkerchief and sneezed. The atmosphere was heavy with the stink of burned cordite.

'That's better,' said Cooney. 'OK, go back to the car and keep your gloves on until you get out of the building.'

Slade's face showed relief at the thought of quitting the scene. Cooney closed the door quietly behind his partner and walked into the bedroom keeping well away from the windows. He dropped to his knees and crawled into the wardrobe below the field of the hidden camera. He reached up, removed the film cassette and closed the panel again. He left the sitting-room as it was, the empty whisky glass on the floor. He made his way down to the furnace-room without seeing anyone. The small sealed box was in his trenchcoat pocket. Outside the wind had dropped and the mist from the river was denser. He opened the Jaguar's door and took his seat, glancing at his partner.

'All right, Dave?'

Slade's voice was shaky. 'Shit, no! What do you

take me for?'

Cooney held the box under the light from the dash and broke the seals with his thumbnail. He lifted the lid on twenty paper-wrapped packets of diamonds. The number of carats contained in each packet was written on the outside. Cooney tore the paper. The loose stones in his palm shone with dazzling brilliance, creating their own colour and fire. Each diamond was gem quality. He put the stones back in the box and turned off the light.

'Does that make you feel any better?'

Emotion made Slade's voice unstable. 'How much do you think, Terry?'

'I don't think, I *know*,' said Cooney. 'There's over a million pounds here.'

The sum was too large for Slade's mind to deal with. Sudden doubt clouded his exaltation.

'How do we know they're not fake?'

Cooney smiled reassuringly. 'Because I know what was paid for them. Five million, six hundred thousand Dutch guilders. OK, we're not going to get that much for them because everyone's got to earn, right?'

'Right,' Slade agreed. 'So how much do you reckon?'

'Eight hundred grand in readies. These people already know what they're buying, Dave. There'll be no messing. We deliver the goods and they produce the cash. It's as simple as that.'

Slade struck fist into palm, overcome by it all. 'Godammit, Terry, we did it! Know what you are, you're a genius.'

Cooney tapped the side of his head. 'I know what I'm doing and that's even better than being a genius. What you've got to do is get that other stuff out of your head, Dave. Nothing happened up there. Nothing at all. All right?'

The memory of the shot, the shock of seeing the pilot's body fall with his skull shattered was rapidly fading. Slade saw sense in what Cooney was saying. He fiddled his fingers, beset by this new feeling of possession.

'You're sure of these buyers?'

'I'm sure,' said Cooney. 'I've brought you this far, haven't I? I just told you: we make the delivery and cop our money.'

'Eight hundred grand.' There was reverence in Slade's voice.

'In cash,' said Cooney. 'And it's going to be there waiting for us. These are serious people, Dave. Reliable. But we're taking no chances.'

'Hell, no!' Slade agreed hastily.

'It's foolproof,' said Cooney. 'The guy who owns the gear can't make a move. He can't scream and he can't have a go at us.'

Slade saw it all in a flash of revelation. The details were somewhat obscure but his own role was clearly in focus. Venom flooded into his voice.

'I can't wait to see that bitch's face when I wrap the mortgage papers round her neck. She can have the house and the payments.'

'Forget her,' said Cooney. 'Get her out of your head. All that's over and done with, Dave. This is a new life.' He reached across and handed the radiophone to his partner. 'You'd better call in.'

The Serious Crimes Squad worked out of undesignated police stations. The task force of one hundred and fifty men were divided into autonomous teams, each responding to the Divisional Commander at New Scotland Yard. The force had its own communications network.

Slade identified himself. 'What's happening, Jock?'

'Not a lot this end,' the despatcher replied. 'How are things out there?'

'Terrible,' said Slade. 'Another wasted day. We've been sitting here with our belly buttons touching our backbones and not even a sandwich in sight.'

'My heart bleeds for you. Will that be all?'

'You're an unfeeling prick,' Slade replied. 'Over and out.'

He looked at his partner and started to sweat again. The notes Cooney and he had written contained a fictitious account of an observation maintained on a house in Highgate, seven miles away. The stake-out was supposed to be the result of a tip supplied by a stool pigeon. There was no danger that this would be checked. The identity of an informer was sacrosanct, respected alike by colleagues and judges.

'You're doing well,' Cooney said approvingly.

Slade wiped his neck. 'Hadn't we better get out of the area?'

'There's plenty of time,' said Cooney.

Slade smiled in the half-light, admiring his partner's coolness, resentful of his own lack of it. 'Don't worry about me,' he blustered. 'I'm not going to make any stupid mistakes, not now.'

'Good,' said Cooney. 'You're still going to do what you said, sweat it out?'

'That's right,' said Slade. He had thought of little else for the last two days. 'Another twenty months and I'm finished. I'll take their pension and piss off, another failed inspector. Then no-one will hear of me ever again, at least not in this country.'

Cooney looked at his watch and then leaned back comfortably. 'I'm too young for all that. I've got my life to live. I know a guy who works for the German State Lottery. He'll say that I had a big win and I'll tell them to stick their job in their ear.'

'It's all right for you,' said Slade. 'You've got no time in. I've got twenty-two years. I'm entitled.'

Cooney grinned. 'It's just as well, Dave. It wouldn't do for both of us to leave at the same time. The main thing is to watch the spending. You know what these bastards are like. They're jealous.'

Slade had a quick sense of power as though the money was already in his pocket.

'I can look after myself,' he said with sudden assurance.

Cooney turned the ignition key. They travelled east along dismal roads still thronged with Saturday night shoppers. They were in Battersea now. Cooney drove to where the Ford Escort was parked. The two men walked across to it. Cooney gave the keys to Slade who settled himself behind the steering column. He belched, bile flooding his mouth. One thing he'd be able to do now was get his ulcer fixed instead of waiting for a National Health Service bed. The prospect of power was tantalising. He raced the engine and turned on the lights.

'Which way are we going?'

Cooney pointed ahead. 'Battersea High Street. And slow when we get there. We've got some cross-country to do. We're going in the back way.'

He wound down his window, picking out land-marks as they turned into a network of narrow streets leading towards the river. They were in the hinter-land between the high-rise tower blocks and the deserted warehouses. Derelict cranes sagged on the crumbling wharves. The buildings were rat-infested, the windows smashed. Battersea Bridge was a watery gleam half-a-mile away.

'Left here,' said Cooney, leaning out further. 'See those lights ahead? That's the back way into the flats.'

They were traversing a building-site. Earth removers had gouged out a track. The Ford skidded through the mud. Slade struggled with the brakes and the steering wheel.

'Where the fuck are we going?' he muttered.

'Watch what you're doing,' Cooney said sharply. He was leaning out of the window.

The Ford slithered on. 'Get into bottom gear,' ordered Cooney. 'There's a gate ahead that I'll have to open.'

Slade could see little. Headlamps battled with the wisps of mist. Cooney withdrew his head and took a torch from the glove compartment. He extinguished the headlamps and shone the torch through the open window. A powerful beam probed the darkness.

'Watch your step here,' he warned. 'There's too much at stake for a cock-up. I'm going to see you through the gate with the torch. Once you're through, turn the car round so that you're facing in the opposite direction. And keep the lights off. I'm going to do the last bit on foot.'

Slade's eyes found the gun in the glove compartment. He nodded. 'Sure you don't need that?' His future lay in the box in Cooney's pocket.

'Nothing's going to happen to me,' Cooney said quietly. 'Keep your eyes on the torch.'

He turned his collar up and released the door catch. Slade watched him as far as he could see into the murk and heard the sound of a gate being opened. The flashlight signalled him on. He set the car in motion again, seeing no more than the beckoning blur of light. He followed it through the open gate. The front end of the car dipped suddenly, all four wheels spinning as the Ford left the edge of the excavation and plunged into space. Slade's last conscious memory was of blinding brightness as the torch was trained on the car from above.

Cooney slithered down the bank and ran to the overturned Ford. It had landed on its side twenty feet below with the driving seat uppermost. Fire was what he had feared most, but there was no leakage of petrol. The engine had stopped. Steam hissed from the punctured radiator. The windscreen was a fine web of shattered glass. He shone the light on his partner. Slade's body was suspended in the seat-belt. His arms dangled loose. The impact of skull against dashboard had peeled his forehead to the bone. His eyes were shut but he was still breathing, blowing bubbles into the blood that covered his face.

Cooney opened the door and wedged himself in behind Slade. Grabbing his partner's head with both hands, he broke Slade's neck with three powerful wrenches. Slade stopped breathing immediately. Cooney took the safety-razor from his pocket and, supporting the sagging head, he scraped off Slade's wispy moustache with the razor. Then he clambered out of the capsized vehicle. The Ford had been rented in Slade's name and the bag in the boot contained a complete change of clothing in his size. A false passport bearing Slade's picture was in the jacket of the suit together with a ferry ticket from Dover to Calais. Cooney took a two-carat diamond from the box and stuffed it into Slade's waistcoat. Slade's head lolled at a grotesque angle, almost resting on his shoulder.

Cooney replaced the ignition keys and climbed back up the slope. He walked towards the river which was still shrouded in mist. He heeled the razor into mud and threw the gun as far as he could. He heard it hit the water and walked away briskly in the direction of Battersea Bridge. A bus took him to Beaufort Street. A lighted sign hung over a door:

RADNOR STUDIO APARTMENTS

He let himself into the quiet hallway. A few letters occupied pigeon-holes over a table. The so-called studio flats were no more than furnished rooms with two communal bathrooms and a washing-machine in the basement. A pay-phone hung at the bottom of the stairs. Cooney let himself into a second floor room overlooking the street. There was a blind with a cannabis plant design, a Kay Nielsen print over the bed and a built-in cupboard with a stout lock. Cooney had rented the room two weeks previously, giving a false name and paying a month in advance. The Welshman who managed the house lived off the premises. Cooney picked his times for coming and going and rarely saw any of the other tenants.

He lowered the blind. He was six miles from his sister's home and knew nobody in the neighbour-hood. A man could drop dead in a place like this and not be discovered until rent day came round. The hallway and stairs were Hoovered once a week and tenants were responsible for cleaning their own rooms. He locked the box of diamonds in the cupboard and went down to the street. He used a call-box at World's End, half-a-mile away.

'Which service, please?' The voice answered promptly.

Cooney had his hand over his nose. 'Police.' The connection was made. 'A man has been killed in Rivermead Court, Putney. Flat L.'

He cradled the receiver quickly and ducked out into the drizzle. Emergency calls were recorded. He made his next call from Sloane Square.

'I'm at Putney Bridge. There are police cars and an ambulance outside Rivermead Court. Somebody else is answering Guerin's phone. I don't like the look of things.'

'That means you haven't made the pick-up?'

'Of course I haven't made the pick-up! I want to know what's happening.'

The line went dead for a few seconds. Then the voice was back.

'Hang up and call me in a couple of minutes.'

When Cooney rang up again the answering voice was agitated. 'There are people in the flat. I could hear them talking. The man who answered the phone asked my name.'

'You didn't give it to him?'

'I made out it was a wrong number. You've got to find out what's happening.'

'OK,' said Cooney. 'I'll get back to you.'

He gave it a quarter of an hour then redialled. 'Guerin's been shot. It's just come over the police radio. What do you want me to do?'

'Is there any way you can get into the flat?'

Disbelief sounded in Cooney's voice. 'Get into the flat to do what exactly? The place is full of coppers.'

'You've got to get in there somehow,' the voice insisted. 'There's a box in the safe. I need it.'

'Hold on,' said Cooney. 'You're not making sense.'

'Guerin keeps the key to the safe on a chain round his neck,' the voice urged. 'I'll make it worth your while.'

Cooney leaned into the phone. 'Have you any idea at all what you're saying? A man has been killed and

15

the police are there. You're asking me to take a key from the body and open his safe?'

'You get in there somehow!' The voice took on an edge. 'I want to know if that safe has been opened. *I have to know if the safe has been opened!*'

Cooney took the right amount of time for reflection. 'I'll do what I can, but I'm promising nothing. Just stay where you are and I'll call you back later.'

Cooney returned to the rented room. He opened his door and stretched out on the bed in the darkness. His plan was working perfectly so far. It was his duty weekend. He'd go to work in the usual way in the morning. When Slade failed to appear Cooney had his story ready. He'd dropped his partner off the night before, Slade having refused the offer of a lift home. Slade had asked Cooney to take the car. Slade's marital problems were no secret. Cooney had assumed that Slade was spending the night elsewhere. Someone would call Slade's wife who would say that he hadn't been home all night. The Serious Crimes Squad was run on liberal lines. Nothing more would be done until Monday morning. By that time the Ford would have been found and phase two would be put into action.

An hour went by. Cooney swung his feet to the floor and stood at the door until he was satisfied that the coast was clear. He returned to the pay-phone at World's End.

'I managed to get up there,' he said guardedly. 'The Heavy Mob's gone and Forensic's installed. I know one of the photographers. I told him I'd been cruising the area and that I'd heard the broadcast.'

'How about the safe?'

'Empty,' said Cooney. 'It's wide open with the key in the lock. Mitch said that it was like that when they got there. But they missed the camera. I managed to cop the cassette.'

'I want it,' his caller said sharply. 'Where are you now?'

'I'm still in Putney,' lied Cooney. 'I've only just this minute left the flat.'

'I need the cassette. Can you bring it here now?'

'I'll be there in half-an-hour,' promised Cooney.

He took a taxi back to where they'd left the Jaguar and drove on to Holland Park. The mansions had been built at a time when servants were plentiful. Most of them had been converted into flats for the affluent. The house that he wanted was halfway up the hill facing the park. The trees in the front had a hundred years' maturity. He climbed the steps and rang a doorbell. He had been there on eight previous occasions, delivering whatever Guerin passed on. The visits were always arranged in the same way. Someone would call Cooney's home and leave a message, stating a time and a day. Cooney would go to Rivermead Court where Guerin gave him a package. The package was always heavily sealed and no-one referred to its contents. Cooney had guessed that he was carrying some form of contraband. He knew that it wasn't dope. It had taken him six trips to Amsterdam to discover the nature and source of the operation. Guerin had never known that he was being tailed. It was Guerin who had warned him that this was to be the last run. Cooney had guessed and guessed well.

A voice sounded in the entryphone. Cooney gave his name and the door opened. The man standing on the right of the hallway peered at Cooney anxiously. He was a short man with the head of a Roman senator. His well-tailored suit and Sulka linen created an impression of dignified prosperity.

He led the way into a room with a ceiling adorned with plaster casts. Brass bars held the white-painted shutters in place and Bokhara rugs glowed on the parquet floor. The furniture was clubland leather. Logs burned in the Adam fireplace.

Cooney removed his trenchcoat and held out the cassette. 'I still don't know what the hell's going on, Mr Dragoti.'

Dragoti's breathing was laboured, his eyes like chestnuts suspended in glycerine.

'How did you get this?'

Cooney shrugged. 'It wasn't difficult. In fact it was Mitch who showed me the safe. They were guessing what Guerin had kept in it. They were all over the place taking photographs. Someone called Mitch and I was alone in the bedroom. I took a chance and as it turned out there were no problems.'

Dragoti opened a door in the panelling, speaking with his back to Cooney.

'Who is this Mitch you keep talking about? Can you trust him?'

Cooney's wave dispelled the last question. 'I've known him for years. If you're thinking about the safe, forget it. A man's been killed, Mr Dragoti. Those people are serious. If Mitch says that safe was empty you can bank on it.'

Dragoti wheeled out a video machine and slotted in the cassette.

'So what are they saying, what do they think?'

Cooney moved nearer the fire. 'Murder to start with. That's obvious. The opinion seems to be that it's something to do with drugs. I just played dumb.'

Dragoti pressed a couple of buttons. Both men watched as a picture formed on the screen. The date and time were super-imposed on the image. The first frames showed no more than the interior of the cupboard, the shelves of shirts and the hangers. Then Guerin's head appeared in profile. He slid back the panel and unlocked the safe. He placed the box in the safe and relocked it. The light went out and the tape stopped turning. When it started to roll again the time shown was two hours later. Now it was Slade on screen, the sweat on his face distinct as he opened the safe and removed the box. Dragoti switched off the machine. His voice was hoarse in the sudden silence.

'Who is this man?'

Cooney made a gesture of defeat. The speed he had stoked himself with was running shafts of light through his brain.

'This is incredible. The bastard! I can't believe it!'

'Who is it?' Dragoti's voice was near to a scream. His face had turned a dangerous colour.

Cooney shook his head. 'It's Dave Slade, my partner.'

Dragoti felt behind him blindly, groping for the chair. He sat down heavily.

'I don't want this double-talk, Cooney. What's going on?'

'I'm trying to get this together,' Cooney said desperately. 'For God's sake, this is as much of a shock to me as it is to you!'

'I want to know,' said Dragoti. His eyes never left Cooney's face. 'There were a million pounds worth of diamonds in that box.'

Cooney took his time lighting a cigarette, feigning a shaking hand.

'That was my partner. I left him at six o'clock. He said he had things to do. I told him I was going back to my sister's place. That's the last I saw of him.'

Dragoti was blowing hard. 'That man robbed the safe. How could he know what was in it unless someone told him?'

A log subsided in the fireplace. Sparks corruscated in the chimney.

'I don't know how he knew,' Cooney said quietly. 'And I don't like the turn this conversation's taking.'

Dragoti struggled up in his chair. 'I want you to listen to me very carefully, Cooney. That box represents everything I have in the world. If I don't get it back, I'm going to pull the house down on everyone. I want those stones back and if I have to find help, I know where to look for it.'

Cooney jutted his jaw. 'You're not trying to blame this on me, are you?'

'Let's not fence,' warned Dragoti. 'This man has stolen my property. Where did he get his information? How could he know about Guerin? How could he know about anything?'

Cooney was sure of himself. 'Guerin must have had some idea what he was carrying.'

'And you?'

'I'm not an airplane pilot,' said Cooney. 'I was getting paid three hundred quid a trip. I was told that it wasn't dope. It was all I knew and all I cared. I kept my end of the bargain. Guerin's your answer.'

Dragoti gave the idea some thought and dismissed it. 'That's impossible.'

'Look, I don't know your business, Mr Dragoti.' Cooney spoke with quiet reason. 'I don't even want to, but you're putting me slap in the middle and someone's been killed. If we don't use our heads we'll all be involved here.'

Dragoti was a broken man. It showed in his face and his voice.

20

'I'm a sick man, Cooney. That money is my future. I have to get those diamonds back. I'm sorry about Guerin, but I must have them back.'

Cooney lifted a hand. 'We've got to stay cool. All this other stuff's going to get us nowhere. We have to work things out logically, Mr Dragoti. Let's suppose that Guerin and Slade were in this together, OK? Hang on, let me finish! They're in it together, right? But Slade has ideas of his own. He wants the lot. So he kills Guerin and reports the murder. As far as he's concerned, I'm still sitting up in my sister's place, three hundred yards away from a police radio. Slade's expecting me to turn up at Guerin's place, ring the doorbell and be greeted by the Murder Squad. That isn't going to look so good for me, is it?'

Dragoti blinked hard. 'But you went there in any case.'

Cooney nodded and came close to the other man. 'Yes, but I knew what had happened. That's the difference. I tell you, Slade's buying time. The police have got no idea at all as to who hit Guerin. The more confusion there is, the better it is for Slade. Don't you see that?'

The telephone rang. Dragoti answered with a show of secrecy. 'I can't talk now,' he said. 'I'll speak to you later.'

He looked up at Cooney, uncertainty in his eyes. 'I don't know what to believe.'

Cooney wagged a finger. 'I'm your only hope, Mr Dragoti. Believe me! I know where to find Slade and I know how his head works. I can get your diamonds back, but I'm through running errands. It's going to cost you real money.'

Dragoti cleared his throat. 'How much?'

'A hundred thousand pounds,' said Cooney. 'No

promises. You get your diamonds. I get my money.'

Dragoti remained unconvinced. 'But he'll know what he's got by now. He's not going to part with it.'

Cooney extended a hand. 'Give me the cassette.' Dragoti hesitated. 'The cassette!' Dragoti surrendered it reluctantly.

Cooney dropped the cassette in his pocket and picked up his trenchcoat. Then he played the card from up his sleeve.

'This bastard's cunning, but he's not as smart as he thinks. Guerin never told him about the camera. What we've got here is enough to convict him of murder.'

Raven

Raven was still in the bath when the phone began ringing. He was just lying there, his mind wandering, the houseboat lifting on the rising tide. It was late afternoon with November misery closing outside the windows. He wrapped himself in a towel and went through to the bedroom. Patrick O'Callaghan was on the line. He spoke in a way that for him was nervous.

'When can I see you?'

Raven sat up hastily. A wet patch was spreading on the Liberty silk bedspread that Kirstie had recently bought. He stuffed the towel under his buttocks.

'What's the problem, Patrick?'

'I can't talk on the phone,' said the lawyer.

'Where are you now?'

'I'm at home.'

'I'm in the bath,' said Raven. 'Give me a chance to dry off and I'll be over.'

He pulled on a sweater and jeans, laced up his sneakers and grabbed the mackinaw Kirstie had brought back from Canada. He had spent the day in bed, reading the Sunday newspapers. His wife had gone to the studio.

The superstructure ran the length of the converted barge with a couple of feet free deck space on each side. Chrysanthemums were growing there in cut-down beer barrels.

Raven's Paul Klee, a prized possession, hung at the end of the long sitting-room. He had bought it at the same time as the *Albatross*. It had survived two assaults on the boat by arson and gunshot and Raven had grown to think of it as a kind of talisman. The shelves beneath the painting held the Raven collection of tapes and records. A colour photograph of him taken by Kirstie the previous summer stared from its silver frame. It showed him deeply tanned, his hair bleached by sun and sea, wearing a look of pleasant befuddledness. The furniture in the room was a combination of styles. The deep chintz-covered sofa and armchairs had come from Raven's parents' home, the fruitwood table from Ontario. Like the sofa and chairs, the much-darned Aubusson was a relic of Raven's family. It was a lived-in room that was cool in summer and warm in winter, a room in which some of the best and worst moments in Raven's life had been passed.

He scribbled a note for his wife and propped it against his picture. He touched a switch, activating the motor that ran the heavy curtains along their rails. Barbed wire looped the top and sides of the door at the end of the gangway. Raven knew only too well that there was little to be done to foil a man bent upon illegal entry. The wire merely delayed him, made things more difficult. He climbed the stone steps from the jetty to the Embankment.

O'Callaghan lived three hundred yards away in Old Church Street. The house was a Queen Anne replica tucked away in a courtyard between Baxter's Rare Books and the Rawalpindi Curry House. The house was built of soft red brick, the door and window-frames painted white. High walls on either side afforded privacy and there was enough room in the courtyard to park a car.

The lawyer opened the door, pressed Raven's hand and hurried him inside. A carved wooden statue of an Aztec rain god stood at the foot of the elegant staircase. The gloss of white paint reflected a brass-bound chest, Hogarth prints and the apricot glow of the carpet. O'Callaghan led the way into the sitting-room. The chairs and the half-circle sofa were upholstered in burgundy leather. An antique figurine of a Russian court dancer posed on a pedestal.

The lawyer poured Scotch into a couple of tumblers. He lifted his glass perfunctorily.

'Something's come up, John, and I'm not too sure that I like it.'

'Tell me,' said Raven. The room was no more than twenty yards from the street but it might have been twenty miles. The courtyard had the peace of a cemetery. O'Callaghan used a match on a Sullivan Powell Egyptian, holding the flame well away from a moustache singed in previous manoeuvres. He was a small feline man with errant hair and lively eyes. He was wearing an Edwardian smoking jacket over his suit trousers and black shoes with tassels.

'A client of mine has been killed,' he said. 'Murdered, in fact.'

Raven was no stranger to death but the announcement disturbed him.

'I'm sorry about that. Is it someone I knew?'

O'Callaghan smoked without inhaling, holding the cigarette like a pen.

'You didn't know him, no. It's a man called Peter Guerin, a pilot with British Airways. He called me last night from Heathrow. He'd just flown in from

Amsterdam and wanted an appointment for Monday. A detective from Scotland Yard turned up here a couple of hours ago. He said that Guerin was shot in his flat last night, shortly after he got home. Shot in the back of the head.'

Rain tapped on the windows, accentuating the comfort of the room. The two men were friends of long standing, accustomed to understood silences. It was Raven's first drink of the day and it fired his stomach.

'That doesn't sound good,' he said, putting his glass down.

The lawyer dropped ash on the carpet and rubbed it in with his foot.

'The man who came, some inspector, said that the police have finished in Guerin's flat and he gave me the keys. I'm Guerin's executor. It's a grisly business, but I have to go there. I'd like you to come with me, John.'

'Of course I'll come, but there has to be more to it than what you've said. I can tell by the crafty look on your face.'

The lawyer felt along his cheekbone. 'You're right. There is more to it. The trouble is I don't know how much. The man said that there's a safe in Guerin's bedroom, that it was open and empty when he got there. They want to know if he kept anything of value on the premises. The whole idea is absurd. I didn't even know that he *had* a safe! As far as I'm concerned he was a client with house trouble.'

Raven replenished his glass. 'How did the police make the connection between you and him?'

'There were letters from me in his desk. All to do with the house. It was rented to people who were creating problems.'

Raven lit a Gitane. 'I'm not sure that I'm the best person in the world to have around when the police are involved.'

'I told you, they've finished. The place is empty. And in any case you're with me. I'd like you to come, John.'

'When, now?'

O'Callaghan nodded. They finished their drinks and called a radio cab. O'Callaghan talked about Guerin as they drove. A mutual acquaintance had introduced them three years before. The pilot proved to be an edgy sort of individual given to making out-of-hours calls about nothing in particular. But as O'Callaghan stressed there were clients like this and Guerin always paid his bills promptly. In addition, he explained, Guerin had a helpful contact at the Royal Opera House box-office. As far as the lawyer knew, Guerin was sexually straight.

They were nearing the end of New King's Road, approaching Putney Bridge. O'Callaghan glanced through the window, getting his bearings.

'I've only been here once before,' he explained as the cab drove over the bridge. He settled back in his seat. 'I'm finding this hard to take in, John. I mean, you're talking to someone you know today and tomorrow you hear he's been murdered. It's upsetting.'

Raven nodded. 'Do the police have any ideas?'

The lawyer shrugged. 'If they do they're not sharing them!' He rapped on the glass. Will you stop here please, driver?'

The cab drew up in front of a building facing the river. Raven knew the neighbourhood as one popular with show-business people. Ownership of one of the houses along the riverside streets was an emblem of success. The automatic doors opened as the two men broke the beam. A voice came from the desk inside.

'Can I help you?'

A short man rose, dressed in a uniform embellished with tarnished gold braid. The lawyer looked at him.

'My name's O'Callaghan. I'm Mr Guerin's lawyer. I think we've met before.'

The porter's finger travelled a couple of inches in the air. 'Of course, sir! I've got you now! Excuse me a minute.'

An elderly man dressed in long overcoat hobbled across the carpet. The porter chased after him, bawling on the trot: 'Sorry for all the disturbance last night, Mr Ackerman.' The man showed no sign of having heard.

The porter came back, rubbing his hands briskly together. 'That's the gentleman lives opposite poor Mr Guerin. It was bedlam here last night I can tell you! The police were in and out all night.'

'Is the flat empty now?' asked the lawyer.

The porter winked. 'They left this morning. Took the body away in an ambulance.'

O'Callaghan displayed the keys. 'We're going upstairs.'

The porter drew closer. He was clearly disposed to confidences. 'The name's Lambert. I wasn't on duty when it happened. I went off at six, see. The police came round my home and fetched me. Banging on people's doors, they were, disturbing all the tenants. No consideration at all. They was asking questions in the middle of the night. A terrible thing to have happened and to someone like Mr Guerin.'

'What did you say your name was?' asked Raven. He knew the type of old. Garrulous, sly and venal.

'George Lambert, sir.' The three were alone in the

lobby but Lambert lowered his voice. 'You've no idea some of the questions these coppers asked. Personal questions. Like who used to visit Mr Guerin. Did he have men friends, did he have girl friends. Who used to visit him. Was he a pervert, if you please! I told them the truth. Mr Guerin was a nice, open-handed, courteous gentleman. Me, I mind my own business if you get my meaning.' He closed his left eye again.

They left him and crossed to the lift. Raven voiced his thoughts as the cage started to rise.

'That one's a weasel. "A nice, open-handed, courteous gentleman"! I wonder what that's all about.'

The emerged into a corridor smelling of freesias. Rough carpentry on Guerin's front door showed that it had been forced.

The lawyer used his keys and led the way into the sitting-room. The curtains were drawn, the windows shut. The place smelled like a bag of laundry. O'Callaghan found the light-switch, revealing the outline of a body chalked on the carpet. Bloodstains near the head were almost black. The ashtrays were filled with exploded flashbulbs and cigarette butts. An empty bottle of duty-free vodka stood on the table together with unwashed glasses.

The lawyer glanced round the room with distaste. 'Imagine leaving a flat like this! These people are animals.'

Raven straightened a cushion. 'You don't get tested for sensibility. All it takes is to be five feet eight or over and able to salute.'

The scene took his mind back to his days as a cop. The kitchen drawers had been emptied onto the table. Salt, tea and sugar were strewn across the floor. An overturned chair near the window meant that someone had been searching the curtain and pelmet. Raven got himself a glass of water. When he returned to the sitting-room the lawyer was going through the desk. O'Callaghan held up an address book.

'Not a lot of help here, John. Guerin's tenant in Wandsworth, a dentist in Amsterdam and my own number.'

The Gitane rid Raven's palate of the taste of chlorinated water.

'Have you any idea what you're doing here?'

The lawyer smiled. 'I don't think I have, come to think of it. I've never done this before. No-one lives completely in a vacuum. There must be friends or relatives somewhere. Not that Guerin ever mentioned any. Do you ever have presentiments?'

'Me?' Raven turned from the bookshelf. There was nothing there but a copy of *Paris-Match* and Saturday's edition of the *New York Herald*. 'The answer is yes and they usually get me into a lot of trouble. Which particular presentiment are you talking about?'

O'Callaghan's bow-tie had wandered askew. He caught sight of himself in the mirror and put it right.

'I don't really know. It's a feeling I've got. I suppose it's something to do with the way that detective was acting. As though it was Guerin who was under investigation.'

'Probably just his manner,' said Raven.

O'Callaghan put some papers from the desk into his briefcase.

'He said he wasn't on the Murder Squad himself. Just making a few enquiries.'

Raven's attention was drawn to the overloaded waste-basket. He bent down and sifted through the contents. He found a couple of scraps of paper under more exploded flashbulbs. One was an Amsterdam bus-ticket, the other the top half of a page torn from a Metropolitan Police notebook. He smoothed it out. The first four digits of what looked like a telephone number were written in spluttered ink. He dropped the paper back in the basket. The police had been there in force.

He went through into the bedroom. It might have been in any hotel. There was no suggestion of the person who slept there, just a bed, a chair, and a dressing-table. A light inside the wardrobe illuminated a small safe lodged in the wall. It was a sophisticated model. The sort of thing that a woman with valuable jewellery might instal. He ducked his head and stepped into the cupboard. The interior smelled of moth balls. Clothes hung in nylon hangers. He inspected the interior of the safe minutely and found nothing. A sliding panel was used to conceal it. He felt his way along the cedarwood lining, tapping and probing as he went. A couple of drawers were set at right-angles at the end of the cupboard. He pulled them out and explored behind, still using his knuckles. The sound was suddenly different. He exerted pressure and a small square of wood moved slightly. Another push and the panel slid back. He found himself staring into the lens of a video camera mounted on a stand. He pushed his hand in and lifted the camera out. His shout of triumph brought O'Callaghan hurrying into the bedroom. Raven carried his find across to the bedside lamp. The two men examined the camera. Its chassis was fractionally larger than the cassette it was designed to contain.

Raven weighed the unit in his hand. 'I've seen

these before. They're new on the market. A thing like this costs a thousand pounds or more.'

He opened the chassis. The cassette was missing.

O'Callaghan scratched through his hair, his face curious. 'What would he want a thing like this for?'

Raven rose from the side of the bed. 'God alone knows!' He stepped back inside the cupboard and scrutinised the cavity more closely. A length of electrical flex was attached to the metal stand.

'See how it works?' he called. 'You open the door and the light comes on. That activates the camera.'

He replaced the unit and closed the panel again. Then he pushed back the drawers and stepped out, wiping the dust from his fingers.

O'Callaghan had taken his place on the side of the bed, still looking bewildered.

'Why didn't the police find it? You did.'

Raven shrugged. 'Pure luck. Too many people doing the same thing. The safe drew their attention. What I don't get is what it was doing there in the first place. It looks as though your client was a bit of a dodgy character.'

His friend came to his feet. 'Rubbish!' His face was suddenly thoughtful. 'What do you mean dodgy?'

'I'd say he's into a scam of some kind,' said Raven. He found himself warming to the idea and continued. 'He was an airline pilot for one thing. That gives him plenty of leeway. How long has he been with BA?'

'Five or six years. I'm not sure.'

'That's it, you can bet on it! He'd be known at Heathrow. Pilots rarely get pulled going through customs. He could have been smuggling dope, for instance.'

O'Callaghan's expression was horrified. 'You're

not being serious, surely!'

'Why not?' parried Raven. 'That would explain the way your visitor was acting.'

'My God!' The lawyer's horror had changed to anxiety. 'You think they left that camera as a trap?'

Raven shook his head. 'You're a respectable lawyer, for crissakes. They gave you the keys. The camera's back in place. End of story.'

'I don't like it,' his friend said. 'I don't like it at all. Maybe we should tell them about finding the camera.'

Raven switched off the lights and the two men walked back into the sitting-room. Raven sat down on the sofa and pulled out his Gitanes.

'You want to tell the police, call them now.'

The lawyer's eyes strayed to the bedroom door. He seemed to be reasoning with himself.

'You know people,' he said suddenly. 'You could ask a few questions about Guerin. If anyone's heard of him. Don't make it hard for me, John. You know the sort of thing I mean.'

Raven was enjoying himself. 'I thought you would never ask.'

The lawyer looked at the blood stains and shivered.

'Let's get out of here,' Raven said quickly.

The blood stains continued to hold the lawyer in thrall. Raven pushed him into the hall and turned out the lights. They continued to talk in the lift.

O'Callaghan stared at his friend. 'I can't get that camera out of my mind.'

'Forget it,' Raven said carelessly. 'Think about Kirstie. What's she going to say?'

The lawyer's manner was suddenly tinged with complacency. 'Tell her you're helping me. She won't mind.'

The cage came to a halt. 'Say that again,' challenged Raven.

O'Callaghan opened the doors. 'This is entirely different,' he said, pursing his lips. 'I'll have a word with her.'

The porter was at his desk. Metal-framed spectacles gave him the look of a deranged surgeon. He came to his feet as the two men approached.

'I expect it's pretty bad up there. The police got someone in to repair the door but they wouldn't let me clean up.'

'It's not a pretty sight,' the lawyer allowed. 'Do you know if Mr Guerin kept anything in store here?'

Lambert removed his spectacles. 'No, he didn't have nothing in store. The police asked the same question.'

'How about a car?' said Raven.

'No car. Mr Guerin always took the underground out to Heathrow. Walk up to Putney Bridge Station he would. If the weather was bad he'd ask me to call a taxi.'

'What about the other porters?' Raven was certain that the man was hiding something.

'Lambert's face assumed a look of scorn. 'There are no other porters.' He tapped himself on the chest. 'I'm the only one. Have been for months. They can't get people to work, not for the money they pay.'

A taxi was unloading a fare outside. The lawyer hurried out to claim it. Raven stayed where he was.

'You're sure you don't remember Mr Guerin having visitors?'

The porter leaned closer. 'What did you say your name was, sir?'

'Raven.'

Lambert lowered his voice to a hoarse whisper. 'I'll

be straight with you, Mr Raven. I don't like the police. Never have, never will. And they've got all they're getting from me. But there *was* someone used to come. I can't talk here, you understand.' He glanced round theatrically.

'Where do you live?' said Raven.

'World's End, Chelsea. I'm usually home about seven.'

'There's a pub at the bottom of Park Walk. The Man in the Moon. Meet me there at eight o'clock.'

Raven opened the taxi door and climbed in beside O'Callaghan. 'I'm meeting him at eight. He's got something he wants to sell.'

He dropped O'Callaghan in Old Church Street and took the cab on to the boat. Kirstie was still at the studio. He left at a quarter-to-eight, collecting the cherry-red Saab from the cul-de-sac. He found Lambert sitting with his back to the window wearing an overcoat two sizes too big for him. The only other people in the bar were the two girls behind the counter and a local drunk preparing for action. Raven carried his glass to the porter's table. Lambert beamed greeting.

'Nice pub this. A good class of people.'

Raven cleared space for his elbows. 'Let's get down to business. What have you got for me?'

The porter's smile was arch. 'That depends, squire, doesn't it? How much you think a job like mine pays?'

Raven shrugged.

'Forty-five quid a week, less tax and health insurance. There's a lot of responsibility attached to a job like mine, Mr Raven. Tenants like to think that there's someone they can rely on. Know what I mean?'

'I'm getting a rough idea,' Raven answered. The porter was setting his own laggard pace.

'I respected Mr Guerin,' the porter said soulfully.

'Get to the point,' said Raven. He opened his palm on a twenty pound note.

The porter made no attempt to take it. 'Like I said earlier, Mr Guerin led a quiet life. Not like some others in the block I could mention. No boozing and carrying on, no birds. But there was this one man used to come to visit him. He'd been coming pretty regular over the last few months. Ever since March as a matter of fact. The last time I saw him was six weeks ago.'

'What's his name?'

The sly look was back on the porter's face. 'I told you before,' he said. 'I mind my own business.'

Raven added ten to the twenty. 'Take it or leave it.'

The money vanished and Lambert leaned forward. 'This feller used to come in a white Jaguar. He'd leave it out front on the forecourt. Big geezer, well-dressed. Never said nothing, just walk straight in and go up in the lift. This one time he come I was outside sweeping. Same performance. Straight into the lobby without as much as good morning. I could hear voices coming from his car so I walked across and looked in. I thought he'd left his wireless on. So when he come down again, I said to him "you left your wireless on," I said. "That's the way to get a flat battery!" He goes as white as a sheet. "That's my CB", he says. "It's against the law. Don't you say nothing to nobody!" And he bungs me this tenner.'

'Did you get the car numbers?' asked Raven.

'No, squire, I didn't,' the porter said smugly. 'Why would I take the numbers? Like I said, it was a white Jag, four or five years old and in good nick.'

'Can you remember anything else about the car? Did you see a telephone inside?' A picture was forming in Raven's mind.

Lambert sucked on his dentures. 'There was something under the dashboard but I didn't see what it was.'

'And that's all you remember?'

Lambert emptied the last of his drink down his gullet. He wiped his mouth.

'That's the lot, squire.'

A spurt of adrenalin poured into Raven's bloodstream. Memory recreated an unmarked police car, the radiophone left off the hook, staccato announcements following him across the pavement. He scribbled his telephone number on a piece of paper and passed it across the table.

'Call this number if you think of anything else.'

He used the phone in the other bar. 'I think we might be on to something. A man has been visiting Guerin over the last few months. I've got a hunch that he could be a cop. There's someone else I have to see in the morning. Someone who might be able to help on the drug angle. I'll call you as soon as I have some more news!'

He parked in the alleyway, rain scudding down in sheets, drumming the roof of the car. Then he ran for the far side of the Embankment. The flotilla of boats creaked and complained in the darkness. It was a close but uncurious community. Those who composed it took care of one another's children and livestock on a basis of mutual aid and resisted all moral judgements.

Raven unlocked the door at the foot of the steps and made his way up the greasy planks. Light from the bathroom shafted across the deck. Kirstie was home. He let himself into the sitting-room.

'I'm back!'

She came to meet him, her wet hair tied in a towel worn like a turban. She was still in her work clothes, tight jeans that made her long legs look even longer and one of his button-down cotton shirts. A suede jacket and Weatherall mac were draped over the tote-bag in which she carried her cameras.

She raised her face and he kissed her smile. Her summer tan had faded leaving a band of freckles marching across her nose.

'How did it go?' he asked fondly, enjoying as always a sense of possession and being possessed.

She tucked in a hank of tawny hair, smiling with her eyes as she sometimes did. It was a sign of happiness, he'd discovered.

'Shall I fix you a drink? I was waiting until you got back.'

They had bought the cider-press in Normandy, a solid piece of oak still redolent of apples. A craftsman in Fulham had transformed it into a drinks cupboard. There was room inside to house bottles, glasses and a small camping refrigerator.

She fixed a couple of martinis, using Polish vodka as base. 'That's wonderful,' he said appreciatively. His voice was less casual than he had hoped. 'A client of Patrick's was murdered last night.'

She backed off towards the sofa. 'But that's terrible! Poor Patrick. He must be upset.'

'He is. Somebody shot the guy in the head.'

She listened, tapping her teeth with a fingernail as he talked.

'How awful,' she said when he had finished. 'Who was this poor man?'

'An airline pilot. He doesn't seem to have any

friends or relatives. Patrick's suggested that I make some enquiries.'

She closed her eyes as if faced with some ghastly sight. 'Oh no,' she said. 'Please God, not that again.'

He adjusted the curtains, talking with his back to her.

'Come on, now, it's not what you think. It's just asking a few questions.'

The casual way that she lit her cigarette warned him of what was likely to follow.

'This might be a flight of pure fancy, my darling,' she said, 'but aren't the police better equipped to ask questions than you are?'

Things were going the way he'd expected. 'You're missing the point entirely. This has got nothing to do with the police. I'm doing a favour for Patrick and it isn't that often that he asks.'

She unwound the towel from her head and shook her hair free. She had been growing it since the spring and the damp tresses hung to her shoulders.

'Isn't there something called obstructing the course of justice?'

He made a face at her. 'You sound like a rookie cop. I ask a few questions from people I know. No more, no less.'

She watched him across the room, bringing a tight little smile to bear.

'OK, let me put it this way and correct me if I'm wrong. Wasn't the idea for you to be keeping a very low profile?'

The boat rolled in the wake of a passing vessel. Long practice allowed him to keep his balance.

'You haven't been listening to a single word I've been saying, Kirstie. Patrick wants me to do something for him. It's as simple as that.'

But his wife had not done. 'Tell me something,' she demanded. 'Tell me something in all honesty, John. How many times do *I* ask a favour of you?'

He gave it the briefest thought. 'Repeatedly.'

'Well, I'm asking you now,' she retorted. 'I don't want you mixed up with murder. *Please*, darling!'

He walked into the kitchen and was back within seconds. 'There's no food in the freezer, thank God. It looks as though Mrs Burrows has finally given up.'

Their cleaning lady had been with Raven for eleven years and viewed his marriage with deep misgivings. She had decided for no valid reason that Raven was not getting proper food and had taken to preparing what she deemed to be his favourite dishes and storing them in the freezer. The Ravens fed most of the food to the fish. Mrs Burrows was loyal, moderately efficient and he had no wish to offend her.

He knew from experience that the issue between Kirstie and him was by no means resolved. The fact that her concern was well-founded made it none the less irritating.

He put on one of her favourite records, Errol Garner playing *Misty*. She cocked her head on one side.

'You're not getting out of it like that, buster! Are you really determined to put me through all that misery again?'

He fiddled the tone and the volume till the speakers whispered the melody sweetly.

'You're getting things out of proportion,' he said. 'Ask Patrick if you don't believe me. A couple of questions here and there. I can get around where he can't.'

Her voice matched the bitter-sweet smile. 'You're an obstinate narrow-minded pig and if you get yourself into trouble don't look to me to bail you out.'

He grinned, trying to break her objection. He sensed that the worst was over.

'You mean you wouldn't even send me a food-package?'

She lifted the drying hair from the back of her neck. 'I've been there before, remember. Captain Midnight setting the world to rights. And when he falls flat on his face guess who's supposed to pick him and wipe him off! Only not this time, darling.'

'Will that be all?' he asked pleasantly.

She inclined her head like royalty. 'For the moment. And if we're eating out I'd prefer Chinese. I'll be ready in ten minutes.'

She disappeared into the bedroom. As soon as he heard the noise of the hair-dryer he was on the phone to O'Callaghan.

'I've just told Kirstie and she's not too pleased. You're going to have to get me out of the shit, Patrick. Back me up. It's just a couple of routine enquiries, remember.'

The lawyer's voice sounded full of Stilton and port. 'You know your trouble, of course. You don't know how to handle women.' He put the phone down before Raven had a chance to reply.

Raven woke to the sound of rain beating the deck outside. It was a dismal sound, a reminder of winter. The digital clock at his side flashed silent time. It was just after seven. He swung himself out of bed, grabbed his slippers and robe and visited the bathroom. Tea, toast and Gentleman's Relish were waiting for him on the kitchen table. Kirstie was a coffee-and-grapefruit person. She had collected the newspapers from the box at the end of the gangway and her face was made-up with a little eyeshadow, blush and lipstick. She was wearing the same jeans with a clean check shirt. She pulled away as he kissed her.

'I do wish you'd shave before you do that,' she complained.

He pulled out his chair and sat down. The window was directly opposite the tidewater calibrations marked on the massive granite blocks. Enough light filtered through from the lamps overhead to show that the boat was riding high. Early-morning traffic thundered along the Embankment. Raven smeared his toast with anchovy paste.

Kirstie sat opposite, brooding over her cigarette. 'You know what?' she said impulsively. 'We're back to the same old routine, the mysterious phone-calls and all the rest of it, aren't we?'

She collected her plate and placed it in the sink. The kitchen was her own creation. She had substituted natural pine for the heavy Welsh dresser and made the walls bright with animal prints. She liked to sit there in summer, watching the high-soaring gulls wheel and squabble.

'I said we're back to the mysterious phone-calls,' she repeated.

'No more mysterious than Jerry Soo,' he replied.

'And you came to bed grinning!'

'What's that, a felony?' He shook his head at her. 'It was a perfectly normal conversation, Kirstie. Jerry's checking a couple of things for me.'

She turned her wrist, consulting the blue-dialled watch. 'I have to go. I'm due in the studio at eight. I've got a cab coming.'

He was in the bathroom when the bell rang at the end of the gangway. Kirstie poked her head round the door.

'Are we seeing one another this evening or what?'

'I'm not sure,' he said. 'I'll call you.'

She stared over his shoulder, meeting his gaze in the mirror. 'One last word, John. You attract trouble. You just can't help it. Remember that. I'll be home about seven.'

He heard the taxi drive away with a feeling of relief. There were times when it was better to be alone. He finished shaving and it was after nine o'clock by the time he had finished dressing. He hurried off the boat rather than see Mrs Burrows. His marriage had come as a shock to her. She had always accepted the previous women in his life, seeing their occasional presence as no threat to her authority. Kirstie was different and Mrs Burrows was still fighting a determined rearguard action.

He closed the gangway door behind him. A dreary drizzle dimmed the street lamps that still burned along the Embankment. He waited for a lull in the traffic and sprinted across the road to the Saab. The Disabled Card displayed in the windscreen had been acquired at the time of Raven's varicose-vein operation. No-one had questioned its renewal. Possession allowed him unrestricted parking privileges. He drove to South Kensington and went into Dino's Restaurant. He drank hot chocolate sitting at a window table thinking about the man he would call upon. Edward Henry Taafe had been at school with Raven. For three brief years they had been friends. School finished, they had drifted apart, totally disparate in character. It would be twelve more years before their paths crossed again. Harrow School had produced its quota of rogues but as far as Raven knew he had been its only professional policeman.

At the time of their subsequent meeting Raven was a junior detective sergeant working with the Drugs Squad. It was the era of acid and morphine. There were comparatively few addicts and the wholesale arrival of heroin in the country was a matter of concern to the authorities. Raven's background made him an obvious choice to help track down the source of the latest menace. Indifferent to the moral issues involved, the thrill of the chase set him alight. He eased himself into the Knightsbridge set and started drinking at Esmeralda's Barn. It had taken him six weeks to establish himself as a user, a couple more months to set up his first meeting with a pusher. The venue was The Orangery in Kensington Gardens. Raven arrived ten minutes early and sat on a bench near the entrance. He had recognised Taafe at twenty yards. The Springheel Jack walk and birdlike head carriage were unmistakable. The meeting was strained at first. Each man was uneasy in his role. The deal had been consummated and the two men separated. Raven explained the position to his superiors and was removed from the case. Eighteen months later Taafe was collared coming through customs at Heathrow with a kilo of heroin in a false-bottomed bag. A judge at the Old Bailey deemed Taafe's refusal to name his confederates an act of misplaced loyalty. It was his first conviction but Taafe was sentenced to six years imprisonment. Released, he found himself cured of his habit and with a reputation of being a stand-up guy. His experience inside left him with a paranoiac fear of returning to prison. He now earned his living as best he could.

Raven used the phone in the restaurant. A sleepy voice answered.

'Yes, who is it?'

'John Raven. Remember?'

There was a pause of thirty seconds. 'How could I ever forget? What's on your mind?'

'We might be able to help one another.'

Taafe's laugh was hollow. 'I've heard of more likelier things. What did you have in mind?'

'When can I see you? I'm just round the corner in Dino's.'

'I'm still in bed,' answered Taafe. 'Give me half-an-hour. I'll leave the street door open. Bring a bottle of milk with you.'

Raven bought the milk in Bute Street and walked through the rain to Clareville Grove. Taafe's flat was over a picture framer's premises. Raven pushed the door and climbed the uncarpeted stairs. Dirty windows on the second floor offered access to a flat roof that extended to the mews behind. It was possible for Taafe to enter by Clareville Grove, climb through a window and emerge fifty yards away. Habit still engaged him in the exercise from time to time as an out-of-practice pianist might lift the lid of his Bechstein.

A dirty card was Sellotaped to the door on the landing. A penciled scrawl bore the message *Back in a couple of hours.*

The door opened before Raven had the chance to knock. Taafe's skin stretched over prominent bones. His eyes were hooded and smudged with fatigue, his teeth well-worn. What little was left of his hair was grey and worn flat. His jacket and trousers were stained and baggy. The shoes he had on were nineteen-fifties brothel-creepers with foam rubber soles an inch thick.

He took the bottle of milk from Raven and looked down the stairs.

'The door's locked,' said Raven. 'Relax.'

The one room had a kitchen unit and a shower-stall in the corner. It was shared with a marmalade cat at present asleep on a plain deal table. There were no carpets, pictures or ornaments. The curtains consisted of lengths of unhemmed material. A single bed was jammed tight against the wall with a telephone on the floor beside it. A television set on an upturned tea chest completed the furnishings. Taafe pushed the only chair in his guest's direction and disappeared into the kitchen annexe. He emerged after a couple of minutes carrying a tray with two mugs and a metal teapot. He filled a mug and gave it to Raven. The first taste furred the backs of Raven's teeth.

Taafe reclined on the bed and fitted a cigarette into a holder. 'One thing I know you're not,' he observed, 'a bearer of glad tidings.'

Raven put his mug on the floorboards. 'What I'm looking for, Edward Henry, is information.'

Taafe repeated the word as though hearing it for the very first time. He shook his head slowly and drew on his cigarette.

'About smuggling dope.'

The bed creaked as Taafe changed position. 'When was the last time we saw one another?'

The memory endured in Raven's mind. A summer day a few months before, the flower-barrow in front of Knightsbridge Underground Station top heavy with roses. Taafe had been standing at the top of the steps wearing dark glasses, a plastic bag under his arm. Greeting Raven, he'd drawn him aside and produced a handsomely bound book from the plastic bag. It was a review copy, he affirmed, a chance to buy cheaply. He knew Raven collected books and so forth. The pitch annoyed Raven, knowing as he did that Taafe had been shoplifting. Raven had produced five pounds, refusing the book.

'May, was it, June?' queried Raven.

Taafe nodded. 'It was June. I still read the newspapers, John. Nothing seems to slow you down, does it. Not even marriage. You're incorrigible.'

The man and the room evoked too many memories. Raven was suddenly depressed.

'It's my curious mind I suppose.'

The cat jumped, landing on Taafe's legs. He scratched its neck lovingly.

'I'll tell you what it is,' he said. 'You've got delusions of grandeur. You're too fucking sure of yourself. You always were, even at school. And all that crap about retiring as a matter of principle! You'd have been as dirty as the rest of them if you hadn't had money.'

Raven picked at a stain on his jeans. 'You don't seem to have too good an opinion of me.'

'I don't,' Taafe said bluntly. 'Not that you ever did me any harm. The trouble with you is that you lack compassion. You've got no time for anyone you think is a loser.'

Raven's head came up. 'Not true. If it's the book you're talking about I don't see why copping a fiver should make you feel bad. You could have refused it.'

'There you go! You don't understand, do you? You simply do not understand!'

Raven took his time lighting a cigarette. 'You mean I don't understand your finer feelings. The short answer is no, Edward Henry. You're slowing down on me, losing my respect. Don't make me sadder than I already am.'

Taafe waved his cigarette holder. 'I wanted to get things straight, that's all. We owe one another nothing, John. You want something from me, then I get paid for it, and vice-versa.'

Raven smiled. 'I wouldn't want it any other way. So now that's settled let me ask you a question. Are you still tight with Phil Drury?'

Taafe's nerve might have gone but the protective coatings remained.

'How do you mean tight? I did time for the bastard. And you know what I got for it? A clap on the back and fifty quid. There's nothing in life like having good friends, John.'

'But he trusts you,' said Raven.

Taafe's veined eyelids gave the impression that he might nod off at any moment.

'Drury trusts nobody. That's why he's never been inside and still has money.'

'But you know what's happening,' Raven urged.

Taafe was still caressing the cat. 'Why are you suddenly taking such an interest in what I know, Raven?'

'I like to keep up with old friends,' smiled Raven. 'Of course there is a secondary reason. As I told you before I need information.'

'You're an ex-cop,' said Taafe. 'Worse still you're a trouble-maker. Don't you think I've got any principles left at all?'

'None that can't be bought, no.'

Taafe showed his tombstone teeth. 'How much?'

'Generous rates,' Raven answered. 'What can you tell me about an airline pilot called Guerin?'

'Nothing,' said Taafe. 'Never heard of him.'

'Too bad,' replied Raven. 'You just blew fifty quid.'

The news brought Taafe to his feet, dislodging the cat. He took a few nervous paces.

'What's he supposed to be, a mule or what?'

'I'm not sure,' said Raven. 'That's why I'm asking. Somebody shot him on Saturday night.'

Taafe swung round, his face assuming a look of extreme distaste.

'Do me a favour, will you! Just go back where you came from.'

Raven stayed firmly where he was. 'OK, if you can't or won't answer that question, tell me this. Where's the money being made these days?'

'Now that I *can* tell you,' answered Taafe. 'They're making fortunes all over the place and I'm getting none of it. These Pakistanis have got thousands of acres of poppies nodding away in the sunshine and they've got their own outfits to process it. These people don't need airline pilots to shift it. They've got ships, Raven. They can afford to lose the odd freighter and still make a profit!'

Taafe wasn't lying. Raven saw truth in his face. 'OK,' said Raven. 'What else are they smuggling?'

Taafe hunched bony shoulders. A weight of disillusionment was embodied in the gesture.

'What else is there left to smuggle?'

Raven came to his feet. 'You're quite sure that the name Guerin means nothing to you?'

Taafe placed his hand on his heart. 'Would I lie to you, John?'

'You would.' Raven prised two ten-pound notes from his pocket. Taafe conjured the money out of sight. 'I'll be in touch,' Raven promised.

'Don't bother,' Taafe said courteously. 'In fact you can cross me off your list. I don't like the company you keep.'

The door was closed firmly as Raven went down the stairs. He walked away, resisting the impulse to look back at the windows of the room he had just left.

Cooney

It was morning and Teresa had already left. She usually went to Mass on her way to work. He drank tea under the baleful stare of the mynah bird. His knuckles still bore the scar from its beak. It was raining when he made his way down to the car park. Traffic was bumper to bumper all the way to Holloway. The Serious Crimes Squad was stationed in a Victorian house not far from the women's prison. There was no external indication of its true function. Casual callers were referred to the nearest conventional police station. Cooney parked in the space allotted and walked up the steps into the lighted hallway. His pulse was racing a fraction but the Diludin capsules he had dropped acted as a catalyst, providing a feeling of invincibility.

The plain clothes duty sergeant looked up from the desk. He lowered his mug of tea and swallowed the last of his sandwich.

'You're wanted,' he said, jerking his head towards the sombre corridor. The Department of the Environment had refurbished the squad headquarters. The walls were a bilious shade of green and yellow, the rooms furnished in order of seniority; Grade One Civil Servant gracing the upper orders, Grade Two the lower.

Cooney took his time, hanging his trenchcoat in his locker and checking his desk for messages. There were none. The duty sergeant was picking his teeth when Cooney returned to the hallway.

'Who wants me?' asked Cooney, assuming a look of surprise.

The sergeant was clearly pleased with himself. 'It's only Commander Birley.'

'What's this, a joke?' asked Cooney.

The sergeant flicked his toothpick at the wastebin. 'On Monday morning? No, he's been here half-an-hour. "Just as soon as Detective Sergeant Cooney gets in," he said. "Ask him to be good enough to step along to the Superintendent's office and see me".'

Cooney straightened his tie, his nerve-ends tingling. Birley commanded the Division and normally worked at New Scotland Yard. Cooney rapped on the door and a voice bade him enter. There were two phones on the desk and the obligatory picture of the Queen on the wall.

Commander Birley was a slight man built on the lines of an Italian greyhound. He was wearing a dark business suit and crested tie. His white hair was neatly brushed, his face scraped clean and shiny. An old-fashioned gold half-hunter was propped on the desk in front of him.

'I don't think we've met since your posting,' he said pleasantly. 'Close the door and pull up a chair.'

Once Cooney was seated Birley leaned forward, his manner changing.

'I'm not going to beat about the bush, Cooney. Detective Inspector Slade is dead.'

Cooney looked shocked. 'Dead, sir? I don't understand.'

'A patrol car found him at two o'clock this

morning. They were making their rounds near some building sites, Battersea way. They came across this Ford Escort. It had gone over the edge of an excavation. Slade was dead at the wheel. His neck had been broken.'

Cooney passed a shaking hand across his face. 'I just can't believe it! What was he doing there? Was the car one of ours?'

'Apparently not. The pathologist says that Slade must have been there for at least twenty-four hours. Probably longer. It looks like an accident but we'll have to wait for the full post mortem.'

The directness of Birley's gaze was heightened by the fact that his eyelids were hidden. 'When did you leave him?' he asked.

Cooney pulled himself together. 'About nine o'clock on Saturday night, sir. We'd been on this stake-out over in Highgate. Nothing seemed to be happening so we decided to call it a day. Dave asked me to drop him off in Camden Town.'

'He didn't go home,' said Birley. 'We've established that much. I just had his wife on the phone. She's coming in later. She says she hasn't seen him since Saturday morning.'

'That doesn't surprise me,' said Cooney. 'To be honest with you, I didn't think he was going home. It was his weekend off and I knew how things were between Dave and his wife. I imagined he was seeing some other woman. Not that it was any of my business, of course. Anyway, we just said goodnight and I let him out and that's the last I saw of him.'

Birley scraped his chair back and flexed his arms. 'How long is it now that you and Slade have been working together?'

Cooney fixed his eyes on a point in the ceiling.

'About three years, sir.'

'Yes,' said Birley. 'You'd better give me a resumé of the arrests you've made during that time.'

'Of course, sir. Any particular aspects you want covering?'

'Just the names, dates and offences. Oh and the disposition. You know, sentences and so forth. I take it you know Slade's wife?'

'I've met her two or three times.' Cooney turned his head away, his feelings seemingly out of control. 'You'll have to excuse me, sir,' he said hurriedly and left the room.

He smoked a quick cigarette in the lavatory and came back wiping his nose. Birley's look showed understanding.

'Tell me something, Cooney. You're a man who speaks his mind. Was Slade an honest cop in your opinion?'

It was time for Cooney to show his true colours. 'Are you asking me if Dave Slade was *honest*, sir?'

'That's what I'm asking,' said Birley. His expression was serious.

Cooney lifted his chin. 'Dave's not capable of being anything *but* honest. It's the man. It's his style. He doesn't think any other way.'

'Did you know that he was up to his ears in debt?'

Cooney picked a shred of lint from his blazer sleeve. Anything to keep his fingers busy.

'I know he owed money, yes. We used to discuss it. But the debts weren't his. They were his wife's. He just got lumbered with them.'

Birley appeared to accept the judgement. 'Things have changed a lot since I first joined. A man with Slade's sort of problems would have been out on his ear.'

Cooney cleared his throat and looked embarrassed. 'With respect, sir, Dave was my partner. I think I have the right to know why you're asking me these questions.'

Birley thought about it, shifting the things on the top of the desk.

'Yes, you do have the right,' he decided. 'A false passport and a complete change of clothing were found in Slade's car. He'd shaved off his moustache and there was a ferry ticket from Dover to Calais. The most interesting thing is that he was carrying a diamond worth eight thousand pounds.'

Cooney shook his head violently. 'You're talking about someone else, Commander. Not Dave. That's just not possible.'

Birley smiled sympathetically. 'Look, I know how you feel, Cooney. But the sad fact is that these things do happen. You can be close to someone for years and suddenly discover that the person you thought you knew well is a total stranger.' He gave the impression that he was speaking from experience.

'But I *worked* with the man!' It was a complete exoneration the way Cooney said it.

'Listen to me,' said Birley. 'Get this into your head for once and for all. Slade was definitely bent. There can be no doubt about it.'

Cooney's manner conveyed grief stoically endured. Behind it a sense of euphoria was lifting him high on wings. He had this clown eating out of his hand.

'It's even worse for me than it is for you,' said Birley, commiserating. 'Remember I started this outfit. Every man in it has been hand-picked by me. That's why we're trying to keep this thing within the division. At least until we establish the facts. We're a team and don't you ever forget it.'

Cooney's glance across the desk was sincere and responsive. 'I've never thought about it in any other way, sir.'

'I'm sure of that,' nodded Birley. 'The trouble is that C.R. Eleven's involved. There's nothing you want to say to me before they interview you, is there?'

The sincerity faded from Cooney's face. The change of pace was disconcerting.

'I'm not sure I understand,' he said.

Birley oozed trust and confidence. 'A man can get himself mixed up in something without even knowing he's doing it. You've got a great record. I wouldn't want to see it blemished.'

'Hold on a minute,' said Cooney. 'What you're trying to say is that if Slade was bent then I must be too. That's it, isn't it?'

'Don't jump to conclusions,' Birley admonished.

'My hands are clean,' said Cooney. 'I've got no guilty secrets to share with anyone.'

The Commander was on his feet, darting from desk to window and back.

'But Slade had!' he said, pointing a finger. 'And it's possible that his wife knows more than she's saying. I want you to go and see her, Cooney. Talk to her. See if you can get something out of her.'

Cooney wanted to laugh in his face. It all locked in tight with the story he had told Dragoti. And here he was being *ordered* to go and see Beryl Slade.

He felt himself smiling ingenuously. 'When do you want me to go, sir?'

The Commander assumed a pose of reflection. 'I'm worried that the press might get hold of her. As far as you're concerned Slade's been posted to Belfast on a mission. That's what we've told them here and it's all you know. As for Mrs Slade we'll have to hope for the best. See her as soon as you can. You could go after Bill Davis has finished with you.'

Cooney's heartbeats accelerated. 'Who's Davis?'

'The man from C.R. Eleven. Don't worry about it. Bill's on our side.'

Cooney shifted his feet. C.R. Eleven was Internal Intelligence.

Birley glanced at his gold half-hunter. 'You'd better clear your desk. If there's anything pressing, give it to somebody else. And go easy on the Belfast story. If anyone asks, you know no more than they do. OK?'

Cooney stood up. He hesitated. 'It's going to be a long while before I trust anyone else again.'

'You'll get over it,' the Commander replied. 'Be back here at ten-thirty.'

The café across the street was empty except for the proprietor, a flabby-fleshed man in a string vest wearing a look of extreme moroseness.

'Tea and toast,' ordered Cooney.

The Italian slid a cup under the urn and opened the spigot.

'No bread yet. No bread, no toast.'

Cooney took his cup to a seat, his mind on the coming interview. His record was spotless. He'd passed up the chances to make easy money. A hundred here, a hundred there. Quick cash for a favourable word to a judge or the chance for a villain to make bail. Cooney had stayed simon-pure, collecting his commendations and moving slowly up the promotion line, waiting for the scam that he knew would come. The big one. Cooney, the man they all liked. Guerin and he had met in a Soho bar. The talk was of far-off places. The pilot knew them all.

Cooney had listened, smiling, his brain alert and receptive. Instinct told him that Guerin was crooked. You didn't go far on a police sergeant's pay, explained Cooney. The farthest he'd been was Torremolinos. Confirmation of his hunch came a month later. Guerin knew of a man who was prepared to pay for a simple service. It was the beginning of something that Cooney had always dreamed about.

He glanced through the steamy window. A Scotland Yard car and driver was pulling up in front of the police station.

Cooney placed some coins on the counter. The Italian swept them into the cash till.

'Your partner no work today?'

'He's in Belfast,' said Cooney. 'Fighting the IRA.'

The man crossed himself hurriedly.

Cooney hurried back to the station. Birley made the introductions.

'Detective Inspector Davis. This is Slade's partner Cooney, Bill.'

Everything about Davis seemed to be a shade of brown. His hair, skin and teeth, his clothing and shoes. His voice was surprisingly soft.

'You've heard the news?'

Cooney sat down. 'I've heard the news, yes, sir.'

'And you know why I'm here?'

Cooney cleared his throat. 'That's obvious, sir, if you don't mind me saying so.'

Birley took up the running. 'As I told you earlier, we're trying to keep this thing under wraps. Inspector Davis wants to ask you a few personal questions.'

Davis sniffed hard. He seemed to have sinus trouble. 'OK, Cooney, what have we got. We've got a police officer with a broken neck in a pit on a building site. He's got a false passport and a diamond worth eight thousand pounds in the car with him. You worked with the man. What do you think?'

Harp strings sounded in Cooney's head. The valuation of the diamond was reassuring. There were twenty packets of them and it was by no means one of the largest.

He lifted his hands. 'I don't know what to think, frankly, sir. I'd have trusted Dave with my life.'

'I've been looking at your record,' said Davis. 'It's pretty good.'

'We've had our ups and downs,' Cooney said modestly. He sensed that he had the man's measure. He adopted a rueful look and flashed the famous smile. 'But that's the way it is if you go by the book.'

The rain-clouds had lowered, making the room darker. Cooney's ear-drums were beginning to buzz, a sure sign that he needed Diludin.

'May I talk to you gentlemen frankly?' he asked.

Birley offered quick reassurance. 'That's what we're here for, sergeant.'

Cooney fixed on a point somewhere in the middle of Davis's forehead.

'I've been with Slade ever since I joined the division. He taught me the ropes here. We worked together, got drunk together and on a couple of occasions we've gone whoring together. I never knew a nicer guy. But there was something about him that you won't find on his record. Dave was one of life's losers. He started to lose the day he met his wife. But none of it affected the way he did his job. He did what he had to do honestly. He didn't have the brains or the ambition to be crooked.'

Davis spoke from within the folds of his handkerchief. 'That's an interesting observation. You think it takes brains?'

Cooney shook his blond head. 'I think it takes the wrong kind of ambition. Dave had none of it. He couldn't see himself as anything else than what he was. He knew that he'd never make superintendent. He knew what his wife was. And there was nothing that he could do about it. I don't care how things look, gentlemen. There has to be another answer.'

Davis looked at the paper in front of him. 'I'm going to ask you some questions, Cooney, and I don't want you getting hot under the collar. You're not the one who's being investigated.'

The questions were not unexpected. They established the details of Cooney's association with Slade, the arrests they had made together, their appearances in court, the villains they had dealt with. Cooney fielded them easily, keeping strictly to the truth. There was nothing to hide. That was the beauty of it.

Davis leaned back, rubbing fingers along his jawline. 'Thank you, sergeant. You've been very helpful. But in spite of what you say Slade *was* corrupt. Everything that you've told me supports that opinion. He was corrupt and clever in a way that you could never have hoped to find out. He conned us, Cooney. You, me, and his wife. What we want is whoever's behind him.'

Birley came in very quickly. 'You're our main hope, Cooney. I realise that it isn't going to be easy for you. The first thing you've got to do is forget about Slade as you thought you knew him. There's every reason to suppose that his death was an accident but we certainly can't be sure of it. Nothing can be taken for granted. You know what's at stake. If we can get to the facts there's a chance of cutting this thing down to size. Beryl Slade is your first point of reference. See what you can get there. I'll be stationed here until this business is settled. You'll report to me personally.'

The three men came to their feet. Davis's nose drew in air sharply.

'It's an unpleasant thing to have happen but you'll get over it, Cooney.'

'Yes, sir,' said Cooney. 'Thank you both for your confidence.'

The station sergeant looked up from his desk as Cooney appeared.

'What the hell's going on in there. Where's Slade?'

'Why don't you ask the Commander,' said Cooney. He slipped into his trenchcoat. 'And while you're at it, you'd better start practising a salute whenever you see me.' He closed one eye significantly.

It was eleven o'clock in the morning but people were still driving with their lights on. Cooney kept an eye on the rear-view mirror. Davis and Birley no longer worried him. His concern was with Dragoti. He left the Jaguar behind Bulstrode Buildings. He climbed the stairs to the flat, made coffee and took it into the sitting-room. Everything in the street looked normal. He picked up the phone and dialled Slade's home number. A woman's voice answered.

'Beryl?' he said. 'It's me, Terry Cooney. I want you to know how sorry I am.'

Her voice had gravel in it. 'Sorry about what?'

'About Dave. I didn't know what to say when they told me. It must have been a shock for you.'

'Anything comes as a shock at five o'clock in the morning,' she answered.

'If there's anything I can do,' he ventured. 'Just let me know.'

'What is this?' she said sharply. 'The Widows After Care Association! I'm glad that the bastard's dead and you know that I'm glad.'

'I was wondering if we could have a chat,' he suggested.

Her hostility was still undisguised. 'You and me have a chat? A chat about what?'

He changed tone and manner completely. 'Something that's in your interests as much as mine.'

'Try me again some other time,' she said carelessly. 'I'm busy at the moment.'

He brought his voice closer to the mouthpiece. 'I don't give a fuck how busy you are. C.R. Eleven thinks that Dave was crooked. And if Dave was crooked I must be too. You've got to help me straighten things out, Beryl.'

'Help you!' She tinkled a derisive laugh. 'I never did like you, Cooney. Your foul mouth or your rotten manners. What makes you think I'd help you with anything?'

'That's simple,' said Cooney. 'If it turns out that Dave *was* bent you'll get no pension. And his insurance won't even pay your debts. What are you and your friend going to live on?'

She was quiet for a moment. 'Nobody's said anything to me about this. I mean Dave being bent as you put it. In any case he paid in for his pension. There's nothing they can do about it.'

'Say you're not sure,' he said. 'If a Board of Enquiry decides he was crooked you won't get a penny. You'd better believe it, Beryl. And I might as well hand in my warrant-card. That's why we've got to talk.'

'Does that Commander know that you're calling me?'

'It's his idea.' Cooney detected the slyness in her tone. 'This thing could snowball.'

She made a sound of exasperation. 'Dave wasn't crooked. He wouldn't have the brains or the guts. Someone must have been using him.'

'Exactly,' he said. 'That's why we've got to talk. It isn't a question of who likes who. It's our asses we're protecting.'

She gave in grudgingly. 'OK. But it'll have to be after four. I've got someone coming.'

Cooney went down to the car park. As he steered the Jaguar out someone moved away from the pub windows. He told himself it was no more than coincidence. He ate in an Indian restaurant. After three mouthfuls he pushed the prawn vindalu aside. His mind was still on the face at the window. The man's movement had been too quick for Cooney to recognise him.

It was a quarter past four when he parked outside Slade's house. It was the last of twelve in the street. Rain rebounded from the tiled roof, swelling the tide on the guttering. A wooden gate opened onto a path running between sodden patches of grass. The last time Cooney had been here Slade had been alone. His wife had been with her friend in Ibiza. The front door opened. The woman standing in the hall was in her mid-forties and beginning to look her age. She was wearing badly-cut trousers and a sloppy sweater. Her hair was severely chopped, her eyes hard and hostile.

He followed her into a room that stank of stale incense. The furniture was cheap and tasteless, the carpet a virulent shade of red. A portrait of a blonde in a polka-dot bikini perched on a side-table. There was no sign of any refreshment. Beryl Slade closed the door to the hallway.

'How much do you know about Dave's death?'

Cooney spoke without preamble.

She lit a cigarette, her back defensively to the wall. 'Only what they told me on the phone. That he'd crashed in a car in Battersea.'

Cooney moved away from the gas fire. His trousers were steaming.

'That's all?'

'That's all.' She watched as he opened a window.

'Then you'd better prepare yourself for a shock,' he said. 'He had a complete change of clothing in the car. Not only that, he'd shaved off his moustache. And that isn't all. They found a diamond worth eight thousand pounds on him.'

'I don't believe it,' she said flatly. 'It's impossible.'

'I didn't believe it either,' he said, 'but it's true.'

She contributed a mirthless laugh. 'Trust Dave to blow it!'

'Dave was an asshole,' said Cooney. 'I've only just realised how much of an asshole. He's been conning me ever since we've known one another.'

She was still watching him, eyes as unwinking as a snake's. 'You know something? You're just about the least charming person I know.'

'Dave was supposed to be my friend,' he retorted. 'And what happens? He's got a thing like this going and I know nothing about it.'

She closed the window again and rearranged the curtains. 'What did you come here for, Cooney?'

'You know why I came here,' he answered. 'Whatever Dave was into I had no part of it. You can help prove it.'

She mocked the idea openly. 'You're the same sort of slob that he was basically. You made a good pair.'

'You must have noticed something,' he said, ignoring her venom. 'Odd phone calls, people who came to the house.'

She laughed shortly. 'You want to know about Dave, I'll tell you. We hadn't slept in the same room for six years. He left the house in the morning and he came back at night. My heart used to sink the moment he put his key in the door.'

'What about other women?'

'You worked with him,' she said. 'Did he talk to you about other women?'

He nodded. 'As a matter of fact he did. He just didn't mention names.'

'Then he was lying,' she said indifferently. 'I don't know what else he told you but he hasn't got it up in years.'

'Maybe not with you,' he said grinning. The drug in his brain found her manner dismissive.

Her face hardened again and she gestured towards the door. 'I want you out of this house, Cooney. Now! And with any sort of luck it'll be the last time I set eyes on you. You're all alike, the whole lot of you.'

He aimed his finger at her. 'You can't afford to throw me out, Beryl.'

She was watching him narrowly. She appeared to be testing his story in her mind.

'Dave wouldn't know a diamond from a cake decoration,' she said suddenly.

He inspected the picture of the blonde at close range. 'Nice legs,' he commented.

She crossed the room deliberately and put the picture in a drawer.

'And where would he get a false passport?'

'Where would he get a diamond?' he said, smiling.

The truth was simple. Cooney had chosen a moment when the desk sergeant was upstairs.

Cooney had taken the key of the Exhibits Room from its place, gone to the basement and removed Beasley's passport from a bundle. Herbert Beasley wouldn't be using it for a while, having just been sentenced to ten years imprisonment. The rest of the work had been done in the locked privacy of Cooney's bedroom. He had substituted Slade's picture for Beasley, the moustache airbrushed out. A heated roller restored the gloss to the paper. The embossed stamp had been difficult to reproduce. Cooney had soaked the original picture in water, superimposed it with Slade's and traced the indentations with the end of a match. Once finished, the passport would have withstood all but a close inspection.

'Believe me,' he said. 'Dave had hidden talents.'

'You're wasting your time here,' she told him. 'You've heard all I know. Once he left the house his life was his own which was the way we both wanted it. If they're going to give me trouble about the pension I know what to do about it. There's nothing I can do for you, mister, nothing at all.'

He picked up his Burberry. She already had the door open. 'Well,' he said. 'This has at least taught me one thing. You don't trust your friends and you don't trust their women.'

'If you do lose your job,' she said from the hall. 'Try selling Bibles. You'd be good at it.'

He stepped through the door to the path. 'We'll talk again, Beryl.'

'Hopefully never,' she said and slammed the door hard.

He sat in the car for a while, trying to determine if she had swallowed his story. The important thing was that he had gone through the motions for both

Dragoti and Birley.

He stopped at a call box and dialled the Holland Park number. Dragoti answered.

'Slade's dead,' said Cooney. 'They found his body this morning. He had one of your diamonds on him.'

'I see.' Dragoti's voice faltered. 'How much do the police know?'

'They're running round like coots without tails,' said Cooney. 'They found him in a wrecked car somewhere in Battersea. My own guess is that he was on his way to a buyer. The stone he had with him was a sample. I've just left his wife. She claims she knows nothing.'

'I see,' Dragoti repeated. 'Do you believe her?'

'I'm not sure,' said Cooney. 'Look, I can't very well talk on the phone. When can we meet?'

'Do you know where Savernake House is? Off Campden Hill.'

Cooney fixed it in his mind. 'Yeh, on the left going up from Kensington High Street.'

'Be there at seven o'clock. Flat number three.'

The stone-built block had a grey marble finish. Number three was immediately on the left of the hall. Dragoti was sitting there waiting. The room was a good example of Ossie Chan chic with the accents on red and gold. The tables and lamp standards were made of pale amber perspex, the chairs and sofa upholstered in Burgundy leather. The one painting was a dramatic rendition of an olive tree seen by moonlight. The parquet floor was strewn with Tabriz rugs.

Dragoti had pulled his chair round so that he could see the entrance to the courtyard. He was sipping a glass of lemon tea. He had aged over the weekend, his neck had become shrunken, his eyelids veined and red. He felt a long way from home without knowing where home was. His tenuous roots extended to Beirut and Paris but they no longer nourished him. His sole source of strength was his family, and Paul was the only one left. The others were either dead or disgraced. Money had always been easy to make in his life, but time had caught up with him. He was tired of the fog and the rain. Most important of all, his heart was tired too. His first coronary had left him afraid and shaken. The years ahead seemed few. It was Paul who had found the answer, an island between Leros and Turkey. It was a thousand acres of rock and red earth. There was only one house surrounded by cedars and figtrees. It was a place to grow old in peace, secure in the knowledge that Paul would continue. The down payment had been made seven months before. The diamonds stolen from Guerin's safe represented the balance.

A Porsche Targa roared into the courtyard. Dragoti put his glass on a table and came to his feet. The front door opened a second later. The man with the key was Paul Zeller, a twenty-five-year-old built like a middleweight. He had strong, handsome features and the grey eyes of his uncle. The looks of a male model were heightened by the pebble tweed suit and brogue shoes he was wearing.

He held his uncle affectionately, chiding him gently.

'You know what the doctor said, you're supposed to be resting. I could have come to Holland Park.'

Dragoti waved his hands, palms down. 'I had to get out of that place.'

There was much about his nephew that reminded Dragoti of his dead sister, the same determination that brooked no control whether the end in view was desirable or not. Dragoti was impressed by the younger man's style and manner. Millfield had turned a whore's son into a gentleman.

Paul Zeller perched on the end of the sofa, showing a length of silk sock. There was no trace of a foreign accent in his voice, nothing about him that was alien to the country of his adoption.

He pulled a set of keys from his pocket and laid them next to Dragoti's glass.

'I managed to get in all right.'

It was Dragoti who had paid for the safe and the video camera to be installed in Guerin's flat, the expensive locks on the door. Prudently he had retained spare keys.

Zeller opened a cupboard and poured himself a glass of apple juice.

'Cooney was telling the truth. At least as far as the state of the place goes. It's a shambles. The door has been broken down and there's blood all over the sitting-room floor. I had a long talk with the porter. Guerin's lawyer's been up there with a man called Raven. The police gave the lawyer the keys.'

Dragoti sought to apply the image and failed. 'Raven? Who's that?'

'Some friend of the lawyer's. He's been pumping the porter for information.'

Pain stabbed Dragoti's chest. He felt in his pocket and found the amyl nitrate.

'What kind of information?'

Zeller's shrug was elegant. 'This and that. The porter's not to be trusted. The thing is, he remembers Cooney. There was this time when Cooney left the police radio on in his car. The porter noticed it. Instead of just ignoring the whole thing Cooney gave the man money.'

'I know about this,' said Dragoti. The amyl eased the cramp in his chest. 'That was months ago. Cooney told me that the car was taken out of service.'

'That could be,' said his nephew. 'But the porter remembered.' He lounged to a cigarette box, looked at his watch and lit a smoke. 'He told this man Raven.'

Dragoti wiped his eyes. Tension affected his vision. 'How do you know all this?'

Zeller allowed himself a secret smile. 'The porter told me. Let's say I persuaded him.'

Zeller's father had been a violent man. Dragoti sometimes saw traces of it in the son. He frowned.

'I wish you'd be careful. We don't want more trouble.'

'We want your diamonds back,' his nephew said shortly. 'I pointed out the danger of too much imagination. Then I gave him a fiver to steady his nerves. Incidentally, he gave me Raven's telephone number.'

'Who *is* this man?' Dragoti demanded. He was getting a picture of something he neither liked nor understood.

His nephew dismissed it. 'He's in the telephone book. He lives on a houseboat in Chelsea.'

'We've got to know more about him,' Dragoti insisted. 'Who does the porter think you are?'

Zeller drew the curtains. 'I wish you wouldn't worry about these things. I said I was the brother of a girlfriend of Guerin's who lives in Holland. I said she was worried about him.'

The answers seemed plausible. 'Cooney's coming here this evening.'

'I was outside his place this morning,' his nephew

replied.

Dragoti's anxiety returned. 'You shouldn't have done that, Paul. He might get the wrong ideas.'

'So what?' Zeller said indifferently. 'He didn't see me. And in any case I don't trust the bastard an inch. People die too conveniently for my liking. The whole thing stinks.'

Dragoti had thought of little else since Saturday night. 'Slade had those diamonds. You can't get away from that videotape.'

Zeller made a show of impatience. 'I've got my own ideas about that. Besides, it's not who took them but who has them now that matters.'

The idea of failure diminished Dragoti completely. He stared at the floor in front of him.

'It's my life, Paul. Yours too.'

Zeller placed his arms around the older man's shoulders. 'We'll get those stones back, Uncle. I give you my word on it. I'm going to do some more checking. I can understand the lawyer's interest. It's Raven who bothers me.'

'My God,' said Dragoti. An idea had suddenly struck him. 'Suppose the porter's told the police about Cooney going to Rivermead Court.'

'He hasn't,' Zeller said shortly. His uncle's plight drew his sympathy. 'Listen to me!' he commanded. 'No matter who or what, I'll always be there. I want you to remember that. No matter *what* happens!'

Dragoti reached up and took Zeller's hand. 'You're a good boy, Paul. Better than any son.'

Zeller put his cheek against the older man's face. 'I *am* your son.'

70

Raven

It was Wednesday morning with the *Albatross* wallowing on the rising tide. The pelting rain of the night before had dwindled to a drizzle that pattered against the windows. It was almost eleven o'clock. Kirstie had been gone for two hours. Raven picked up the phone and dialed Jerry Soo's office.

'Hi!' he said. 'What have you got for me?'

'I'll meet you in half-an-hour,' his friend said quickly. 'The usual place.'

There were no free parking places near the restaurant. Raven left the Saab on a yellow line with the Disabled ticket prominently displayed. Soo was already there, sitting at a window table surrounded by ageing Sloane Rangers. He was wearing a nylon raincoat over a dark blue business suit. Gone were the jogger's suit and the baseball boots. Soo's transfer to C.R. Eleven had curbed the Hong Kong-born cop's style of dressing.

'What did you do, run here?' asked Raven, dropping into a free chair.

Soo offered his wide gold-toothed grin, his boot-button eyes almost disappearing. His skin was the colour of very old ivory, his brushcut hair blue-black at the roots.

'I don't have much time,' he said. 'First thing is

don't call me at work. A couple of guys there can hear round corners.'

He reached inside his jacket and drew out an envelope. He placed this on the table between them.

'You wanted to know about Mark 4 Jags. There are twenty-two of them on the strength. The Flying Squad's got ten, Serious Crimes four and the rest are divisional with the exception of two that are out of service. One's white, the other's grey.'

'Do you know when the white one was taken off the road?'

'May the ninth.'

'Of course it was May the ninth,' said Raven. The porter had been sure of his dates. His birthday had fallen on the date following Cooney's visit and the unexpected windfall had paid for Lambert's celebrations.

Soo continued to stare impassively. 'You're not going to tell me what you're doing, John?'

'It's something for Patrick O'Callaghan. Just a couple of enquiries to do with a client.'

Soo made a sound like a martial arts grunt. 'Don't give me the offhand touch! I know you too well and it doesn't suit you.'

Raven lowered his voice. 'Someone was killed on Saturday night, a pilot with British Airways. Patrick doesn't like the way you people are handling the enquiry. The guy was murdered.'

'I guessed as much,' said his friend. 'And you're looking under the rugs for Patrick. I had a hunch that the damaged car would be the one you were interested in. It was booked out to a Detective Inspector Slade and a sergeant called Cooney. They're both on the Serious Crimes Squad in Holloway.'

Raven opened the envelope. The photographs inside were the type issued for police identification. A name and address was written on the back of each picture.

Raven took a quick look at the neighbouring tables. No-one was listening to their conversation. Slade's likeness showed a man with blurred features, wispy hair and a strawberry nose. The other man's face was framed in longish blond hair. A readiness to smile was indicated but the eyes were cold and watchful. He put the envelope in his pocket.

'Thanks, Jerry.'

'Don't thank me,' Soo said quickly. 'I never saw those things in my life. And while we're on the subject, I put those two in our computer. They came out like a couple of choirboys. Not a whiff of fish anywhere. Twenty minutes later I got a call from one of our hatchet-men, someone called Davis. He wanted to know what my interest was in Cooney and Slade. The computer operator must have informed him.'

Raven was following every word. 'And?'

Soo spread his hands. 'I said that a member of the public had phoned giving the number of the car Slade and Cooney were driving. The man wanted to know if it was a police vehicle because it had been parked outside his house for four hours.'

'Did Davis go for it?'

Soo turned his mouth down. 'Would you? I felt a real clown. He gave me a mouthful about what he called "procedural behaviour" and said that if I didn't like it I could go to the A.C.'s office. That sort of refined my thinking.'

'I'm sorry,' said Raven. He pushed the remains of his croissant aside.

'I'm the one who's sorry,' said Soo. 'I don't like making a fool of myself.'

'Just one last thing,' Raven urged. 'Did you ever hear the name Peter Guerin?'

'No,' answered Soo. He signalled for the bill. 'And I'll try to forget it now that I have. There are times when I find myself wondering why I continue to know you. I can understand how Kirstie feels.'

The waitress appeared with the bill. Raven collected it.

'Everyone understands how Kirstie feels including me. Nobody understands how *I* feel.'

Soo clapped Raven's shoulder. 'No more calls at work, remember. I'll be in touch.'

Raven drove home and parked in the usual place. He switched off the engine and the cul-de-sac was quiet. The windows of *Serendipity* were radiant with tapers and candles. Raven's green-bearded neighbour sprawled in a chair with his feet resting on top of a Great Dane. Man and dog were surrounded by painted and gilded figures, Devil masks and effigies of tiger gods from Java and Sumatra. Raven rapped on the glass as he passed. Hank raised a lazy hand, stoned as usual.

Traffic between the two bridges was solid. It was five minutes before Raven seized the chance to charge for the other side. No-one gave quarter along the Embankment. He picked his way gingerly down the stone steps. He wondered if Kirstie was home yet. He'd done his best to share that part of her life and had failed. The main reason was the people she was involved with. Coke sniffing PR men and advertising agents, models entirely in love with themselves, all plastic creatures of the hype and the media. It was better in Paris, but most of her recent work seemed to be coming from London.

His rubber soles squelched along the wet deck. The ducks were active below, cruising through the weeds that grew on the mud-flats. He unlocked the sitting-room door. It was quiet inside with the roar of the traffic above eliminated by the double-glazing. His hand stopped halfway to the light-switch. He lowered his arm, his senses acute as he turned his head slowly. He could make out the shapes of the bookshelves, the sofa, his desk. Instinct told him that something was wrong. He tiptoed across the room and felt the bulb in the lamp on top of his desk. It was still warm. Someone had heard him coming and had extinguished it. The locks on his doors were the best money could buy but sometimes they failed. Authorised dealers retained the master-keys. A man with the right manner or contacts would have no trouble in laying hands on them.

Raven steadied himself against the wall and slipped off his sneakers. Cautiously he crept into the darkened kitchen and groped behind the wine-bin. His fingers touched the canvas guncase. He drew it out carefully and removed the Purdey shotgun. A box of Rigby Smokeless nestled in a side pouch. He slotted a cartridge into the breech and cat-trod into his bedroom, holding the shotgun short and waist-high. He saw the room clearly, the familiar shape of Kirstie's one-eared bear wedged between the pillows on the cane-headed bed, the flowers on the window ledge, the faded snapshot of his parents in a frame on the dressing-table. He opened the cupboard with one swift wrench, training the barrel of the shotgun on the interior. Nothing moved. Everything looked normal.

He moved crabwise to the bathroom, his shoulder-blades pressing against the wall. Mrs Burrows had left a pile of clean towels on the stool. The glow through the frosted windows changed in intensity as the boat rolled away from its neighbour. Raven inched on to the guest-room. Mirrors dimly reflected his image in triplicate. His nostrils flared, aware of an unfamiliar odour, a scent or cologne of some kind. He was between the two single beds when a hand snaked out from the floor, imprisoning Raven's ankle. The man rose, taking the bed with him. A weight descended on Raven's head. He toppled sideways, releasing his grip on the shotgun. The cartridge exploded, shot peppering the walls and the curtains.

Raven had no idea how long he lay there. The next thing he knew, someone was opening the door leading in from the deck. He groaned loudly, feeling the bump that had risen above his left ear. The shotgun was lying on the floor, half-covered by the overturned bed. The light came on. Kirstie stood in the doorway, sniffing the aftermath of the explosion.

Raven hauled himself up shakily. His wife's fingers flew to her throat. She hurried forward to help him, running the words together in her anxiety.

'My God, what happened?'

He stumbled in the direction of the kitchen, groped for a chair and sat down heavily.

'A drink,' he said, 'anything!'

She yanked open the door of the refrigerator. He pulled the tab off a can of beer and emptied it thirstily. The movement shot shafts of light through his eyeballs.

Kirstie shook her head, staring at his stockinged feet. 'What on earth happened?'

He emptied the freezing department of ice-cubes,

packed them into a napkin and held it against the side of his head. Kirstie followed him into the sitting-room.

'Are you just going to sit there or what?' she demanded. 'What happened?'

Ice-water was running down his sleeve. He put the napkin in a flower-bowl.

'There was someone on the boat when I came back. I knew it the moment I opened the door. But I didn't know where the bastard was, hiding under one of the beds in the guest-room. He clobbered me with a blackjack. I didn't even get the chance to see him.'

She ran into the bedroom and came back with her red leather trinket box.

'Nothing's missing. Not a thing!'

He opened the top of his desk, looking down at the place where he kept his personal documents, birth certificate, passport, souvenirs of his police service. He shut the desk again, speaking with a flash of understanding.

'This guy didn't come to steal, Kirstie. He's been through my papers, that's all.'

She sat down abruptly, still clutching her jewel-case. 'Are you going to call the police?'

He looked at her blankly. 'He must have been going through my papers when I opened the gang-way door.'

'It was a stupid question obviously!' She lit a cigarette and perceived him through smoke. 'Am I permitted to know who this intruder is or do I have to be killed by a total stranger?'

'For God's sake!' he said impatiently. The ice-pack was dripping onto the carpet now. He took it into the kitchen and dumped it in the sink. His head spun as he bent to pick up the shotgun. He found a pair of slippers and sat down beside her.

'I don't know who this man was, but I can make a good guess,' he said.

She blew a smoke-ring over his head. 'That's a start,' she answered. She proceeded to blow one smoke-ring through the other.

It was a trick that was still beyond him after years of secret practice.

'I've been doing something for Patrick, right?'

She nodded. 'That's what you told me.'

He took the cigarette from her fingers and inhaled. 'This guy was something to do with it. No question.'

She leaned back into the nest of cushions, one hand lifting the hair from her neck.

'Why didn't you say so at the beginning. That makes it perfectly fine, including any other horror that might be going to happen to us.'

He shook his head gingerly, exchanging her cigarette for one from the pack of Gitanes on the table.

'Let's skip the sarcasm, shall we? OK, call the police, you say. Suppose I told you that the police are already involved and they're not on our side?'

She stayed as she was, her head thrown back on the cushions.

'That wouldn't surprise me,' she said. 'They never are when we need them. That's what I'm talking about, John. But you're a grown man and there's nothing I can do to change you.'

He managed a smile. 'You don't really want to, do you?'

That brought her up from her nest. 'If that's what you think, you're a klutz! It was different at the beginning. I thought it was a phase you were going through. I must have been crazy.'

He grabbed her hand, forcing her to look at him.

'This isn't some brain-storm, Kirstie. It's serious business.'

She freed herself from his grasp. 'But it isn't *your* business, is it? I told you last year in Portugal. I just can't take it any more. You'll find me at 35 Quai d'Anjou if you need me.'

'Rubbish!' he said. The throbbing in his head had diminished. 'You're not going anywhere. For one thing you're too much of a pro to walk out in the middle of an assignment. You'd lose Maggie Sanchez, a starched monster if ever I saw one, but she packs them in.'

She moved her shoulders, admitting partial defeat. 'OK but I'm about to serve formal warning, my darling. You're my husband and I love you. I'll come to see you in hospital, visit you in jail, but I refuse to help you put yourself there. Is that clear or not?'

'It's perfectly clear,' he said, smiling. 'Do you want to eat something here or go out?'

She rose, ruffling his hair. He winced as she touched the bump on his head.

'Out,' she said, 'but I want to take a shower first. I missed mine this morning.'

He waited until he heard the water running and picked up the phone. O'Callaghan answered.

'It'll have to be quick. I'm on my way out.'

Raven kept his voice down. 'I saw Jerry this morning. That Jaguar that the porter saw at Rivermead Court was a police car. Not only that, it was taken out of service on the following day, I've got pictures of the two men who were using it. I'm going to show them to the porter.'

'Are you sure about this?'

'I'm sure,' said Raven. 'And listen to this. Jerry put this pair through the computer and someone in the

Division stomped all over him. The guy wanted to know Jerry's reasons.'

A hint of impatience crept into the lawyer's voice. 'We'll have to talk later. I'm running late as it is.'

'Stay right where you are,' ordered Raven. 'Someone was here on the boat when I got back. He laid me out cold. Nothing was taken but I'm pretty sure that he went through my desk.'

'Are you hurt?' the lawyer asked quickly.

'Only my pride.'

'Did you inform the police?'

'Don't be ridiculous. You sound just like Kirstie.'

O'Callaghan's voice was doubtful. 'I don't like this, John.'

'I didn't expect that you would,' said Raven. 'I'll talk to you later.'

Kirstie was still in the shower, her long legs showing through the curtain. He adjusted his hair in the mirror so that it covered the lump on the side of his head.

'Can we hurry it up a bit?' he called.

He heard her gasp as the cold needles hit her back. She stepped out of the shower-stall and reached for a bath sheet.

He kissed her bare shoulder. 'Get your clothes on. There's a call we have to make before lunch.'

They sat in the Saab while Kirstie finished her make-up. She rolled one lip over another and put her eyeliner in her bag.

She looked at him brightly. 'Where are we going?'

'Putney,' he said and switched on the ignition.

'Wonderful,' she said, squinting through the swishing wipers. 'What could be nicer on a day like this.'

He set the car in motion, ignoring the remark. 'I've

got to show a guy a couple of photographs. The problem's going to be keeping his mouth shut afterwards.'

Her answer surprised him. 'Is there anything I can do to help?'

He turned into the westbound traffic. 'You'd actually do that for me?'

She smiled at his reflection in the driving-mirror. 'Out of sheer self-defence.'

He winked at her. 'Sometimes I think you're too good for me. Not often but sometimes.'

He took the quick route, across Wandsworth Bridge and over the hill down to Putney. Kirstie spoke little, engrossed in the tape that was playing. In spite of the hour, lights were shining in the lobby of Rivermead Court. Raven could see Lambert standing there, talking to a woman with a small dog in her arms. Kirstie shivered, looking at the leaves sailing into the dark brown river.

'I hate this time of the year in this country.'

'We'll do better next year,' he promised. 'This shouldn't take long.'

He pulled on his waterproof hat and sprinted towards the lobby. The porter saw him coming too late. Lambert managed to reach his desk before Raven caught up with him.

Raven shook the rain from his hat. 'How's everything going, Lambert?'

The porter fiddled the papers on his desk, his manner distinctly uneasy.

'I can't talk now,' he said. 'I've got to go up and see a tenant.' He tried for detail to increase his plausibility. 'Something wrong with her lights.'

Raven barred his way, pulling the envelope from his pocket. He placed the two photographs on the desk.

'Do you recognise either of these people?'

The porter glanced down furtively but said nothing.

'You're going to tell me the truth, aren't you?' Raven said pleasantly.

Lambert's gaze roved round the lobby but he found no help. He stabbed a finger at Cooney's picture.

'This one. It's the geezer I told you about. The one who used to visit Mr Guerin.'

'How about the other man?'

'Never seen him in my life,' said the porter. His eyes sought the wet dismal forecourt. The Saab gleamed like a jewel in the rain.

Raven put the pictures back in his pocket. He cupped the porter's chin with his hand and forced the man's head up.

'Who did you give my phone number to?'

The porter's eyes goggled as he tried to speak. Raven released him. The porter backed off, his glare resentful, rubbing his chin.

'Who do you think you are, coming in here and behaving like that! I've a good mind to . . .'

Raven cut him short. 'Shut up and listen. Who's been here talking to you? Who wanted to know about me? Was it the man in the picture?'

The porter's manner changed abruptly. If he had had a tail it would have wagged.

'He was a stranger to me, a complete stranger! He come in here saying that his sister was a good friend of Mr Guerin's. He wanted to know about Mr O'Callaghan and you. I can't take no aggression, Mr Raven. My lungs aren't that good and I'm under the doctor.'

'So you gave him my name and telephone number.'

Lambert's defiance wavered and broke. 'He threatened to do me up, Mr Raven. I know when someone means it. I can't take harassment.'

'What else did you tell him?'

'Nothing. He was up in Mr Guerin's flat for almost an hour. He had the keys.'

'Do you know this man's sister?' Raven could see Kirstie peering through the car window in their direction.

Lambert shrugged dejectedly. 'I never saw Mr Guerin with any lady. I'm really sorry, Mr Raven. I'll admit it, I was scared.'

'This man, how were you supposed to get in touch with him? Did he leave you a telephone number?'

'He didn't leave *nothing*!' Lambert's denial had the force of the habitual liar who tells the odd truth. 'He just give me this look. "I'll be back" he says and slopes off in one of them sports cars.'

Raven leaned forward, pinning the porter against his desk.

'You and I are going to start all over again. I'm a lot more dangerous than your friend and you'd better believe it. If this man does get in touch with you I want to be the first to know. Understood?'

The porter's eyes slipped sideways.

'And you don't tell him that I've been here,' added Raven.

'I don't tell nobody *nothing*! Except you,' the porter added hastily.

'You're making sense,' said Raven. 'See that you keep it up.'

Kirstie had the car door open for him. 'That was quite a performance to watch,' she said. 'Who won?'

He fastened his seat-belt, looking back at the lobby.

83

'I'm not too sure but I think that I just about got the edge.'

They lunched in the King's Road then Raven drove his wife to the Health Club. It was seven o'clock by the time he collected her. Fulham Road was a nightmare of homebound pedestrians wielding umbrellas like weapons, top heavy buses spraying the pavements with slush. The Saab stopped outside O'Callaghan's house. A yellow Datsun was parked in the courtyard. They hurried into the lights and the warmth. Maureen Hannay took their coats. She was a tall brunette with elegant movements that showed her ballet training. Her smooth dark hair was worn long in a chignon, accentuating her classical bone structure. She was wearing a hand-blocked silk dress of green and yellow. She touched Raven's cheeks with her lips.

'Patrick's in the sitting-room.'

She disappeared upstairs, taking Kirstie with her. O'Callaghan closed the door behind Raven and opened a lacquer chest.

'What can I give you to drink?'

This was a room to relax in. The apple log fire burned brightly complementing the colours of the curtains and carpet.

'Scotch'll be fine,' said Raven.

The figurine of a dancer had come from the Imperial Ballet School in Saint Petersburg. Raven was rarely envious but the cast silver shape was something he wished he owned.

'Are you people going out?' asked Raven.

The lawyer was looking exceptionally spruce for the time of day. Court appearances usually took their toll of his tidiness.

O'Callaghan handed him the tumbler. 'An exhibition. Some painter that Maureen knows. It's our week for culture. *Die Lohengrin* on Friday.'

Raven drifted nearer the fireplace. 'I want you to listen very carefully to this, Patrick.' He told the lawyer what had happened on the boat earlier.

His friend frowned, nibbling his moustache. 'You think this was the same man who was at Rivermead Court?'

'I'm sure of it,' said Raven. 'And what's more he had keys to get into the flat. I wouldn't recognise him if he walked through that door. But one thing's for sure. The man's not particular what he does.'

'And this cop the porter identified?'

Raven produced the two photographs. 'The young one's Detective Sergeant Cooney. He's with the Serious Crimes Squad in Holloway. I get the impression that Guerin was no ordinary pilot.'

Voices sounded on the landing upstairs. 'How much does Kirstie know of all this?' O'Callaghan asked hurriedly.

'Everything,' said Raven. 'And she doesn't much like it. This business on the boat scared her rigid and I can't say that I blame her.'

He broke off as the two women came into the room. Maureen fixed drinks for herself and for Kirstie.

'Have you two finished with secrets?' she asked, smiling. She sat down next to Raven and stared at his trousers. 'You're wet! Why don't you take those off and borrow something of Patrick's?'

'Well for one thing, he's five feet seven and I'm six four. And they're almost dry anyway.'

Kirstie spoke from the fireplace. 'He's daft, Maureen, that's what he is. After all that business last year we're back with the derring-do, would you believe! Only this time I'm supposed to blame Patrick.'

'There are some things that a lawyer's not able to do,' O'Callaghan said urbanely.

Kirstie put her glass down. Firelight gave her the look of a teenager.

'It's back to Captain Midnight, the Scourge of Wrongdoers.'

Raven shook his head at her. 'If you want to embarrass people you're going the right way about it, Kirstie.'

'We can drop the whole thing,' the lawyer said hastily. 'Find some other way to sort things out.'

'We're dropping nothing,' Raven retorted. 'I don't like being clobbered by a total stranger for one thing. Another thing is that I'm starting to enjoy myself.'

His wife rolled her eyes at the ceiling. 'Things don't have to make *sense* for him, Patrick. You should know that.'

Raven ignored her. 'I'm going to see Slade. I've got his address.'

'You're not taking care of your guests,' Maureen chided, looking at the lawyer. She refilled Kirstie's glass.

Raven shook his head. 'A man has been killed,' he said patiently. 'And we know that at least one cop used to visit him. Why did this character jump all over Jerry when he made that computer enquiry? I'll tell you why. They're trying to keep this thing under wraps. No, I'm going to see Slade tonight. I'll say I'm a friend of Guerin's and I want to know what's going on. I know how far to go, Patrick.'

O'Callaghan was wearing his doubtful expression. The surreptitious nibbling of his moustache was part of it.

Kirstie was clearly running out of patience. 'This is ridiculous,' she said to the other woman.

Raven continued to aim his argument at O'Callaghan. 'I'm going to go out there and just knock on his door. No advance warning. Just turn up and introduce myself. It'll get results, I promise you.'

He came to his feet, holding the coat that Maureen had fetched. Kirstie slipped into it.

'Ah well,' she said. 'There's a lot to be said for the simple life. Thanks for the drinks. You people enjoy yourselves!'

Raven kissed the brunette. 'Would you rather I took you home?' he asked Kirstie.

She shivered theatrically. 'With thugs creeping about on the boat? No, thank you!'

Half-an-hour later they were approaching the wet waste of Streatham Common. They stopped at the top of the hill. Raven looked across at the house.

Water was cascading from the blocked guttering. He crossed the street and rang the door-bell. Chimes sounded inside. The summons remained unanswered. A piece of material attached to the mail-flap prevented him from seeing through into the hall. He heard the sound of women's voices. He rang the bell a second time. Light stained the glass at the top of the door. A bolt was withdrawn.

Raven touched the brim of his shapeless hat. 'Mrs Slade?'

The woman was in her forties with strong features and clump-cut hair. She was wearing a man's shirt outside jeans that were too tight for her.

Her voice and manner were uncompromising. 'What do you want?' She stared behind him, locating the car that was parked across the street.

He moved out of range of the falling water. 'Are

you Mrs Slade?' He managed to stick his foot out before she could close the door. 'I think we'd better talk,' he said.

A thin blonde in a candy-striped dress was sitting on the top of the stairs with a telephone in her lap. The other woman looked hard at Raven.

'If it's my husband you want, he's not here.'

Raven pushed into the hallway. 'It's a personal matter.'

The glance the two women exchanged suggested complicity. The blonde was too old to be Mrs Slade's daughter.

'If your husband isn't here,' Raven said politely, 'perhaps you could tell me where I can find him.'

Mrs Slade's voice took on an edge. 'What did you say your name was?'

'Raven,' he said. 'A friend of Peter Guerin's from Amsterdam.' His smile at the blonde advanced nothing.

Mrs Slade added her own hostile glare. 'Peter *who?*'

'Guerin,' Raven repeated. 'It's important that I see your husband, Mrs Slade. Very important.'

She held him as a snake-handler does a cobra, firmly but well out of reach of its fangs.

'As far as I know, my husband's in the mortuary. He broke his neck in a car accident on Saturday night.'

'I'm sorry,' he said automatically. The news had completely confused him.

'Why be sorry?' she answered. 'You didn't know him, did you? I loathed the bastard. And let me tell you something, Mr Raven. I wasn't married to a policeman for nothing. I want you to get out and stay out. And you can tell the rest of your journalist friends. They'll get nothing here.'

She flung the door wide. Raven stepped out, avoiding the fall of water. The door slammed and the light in the hallway went out.

Kirstie greeted him with what was just short of a smile. 'And how did that one go?'

He sat down beside her. 'Slade's dead, killed in a car accident on Saturday night. I *was* right, Kirstie. They're trying to cover it up.'

She looked across at the house he had left. The only light showing was upstairs.

'We've been had,' he said. 'These people are making fools of us.'

She reached across and brought the lights to life. 'So what,' she exclaimed. 'Let 'em get on with it. It's not your concern.'

He twisted sideways so that they faced one another. 'Let me ask you one question,' he said. 'Do you love me or not?'

She looked at him, twisting her wedding ring. 'This is blackmail,' she said.

'Answer me,' he insisted.

'Of course I love you,' she said. 'Not as much as you love yourself, of course. That's why I'm doing my darndest to keep you in one piece.'

'If you love me you'll help me, Kirstie. I need your support.'

She continued to stare for the space of ten seconds. 'You're a bastard,' she said. 'I'd like to go home, please.'

He parked on the Embankment and sat in his seat with the engine running. His wife looked at him briefly and collected her bag from the glove-compartment.

'I get it. You mean you're not coming on the boat with me?'

He shook his head. 'I've got to get hold of Lambert. It's important.'

She opened the door on her side. 'Don't worry about me being robbed or raped. Or both. With the telephone lines cut. I can always yell for help.'

'I won't be long,' he said. 'Dig in the freezer, we'll eat at home.'

There was no-one on duty at Rivermead Court. A woman living in the block told Raven that the porter had not been seen for some hours. She gave Raven the number of the managing agents. The porter's home address proved to be in a street of shabby houses between Lots Road and the Kings Road. Raven rang the doorbell. A woman appeared and he touched the brim of his rainhat.

'I'm looking for Mr Lambert.'

A light burned in the hall. A scarf tied over Carmen rollers gave the woman a witchlike appearance. She wasted no time with niceties.

'So are a few other people, me for one. Who are you, anyway?'

'I'm with Allen and Squires, the agents. Mr Lambert isn't at work. We wondered what was wrong.'

She shuffled a couple of steps nearer. 'I'll tell you what's wrong. The miserable little bugger shoved off in a car while I was out shopping. The lady lives next door seen it all. Like a thief in the night, he went. And me putting up with his filthy habits and giving him the first decent home he ever had. Owes a week's rent, he does, as well. You find him, mister, you let me know!'

She slammed the door hard. Raven returned to the houseboat. Supper finished, he told Kirstie about the porter's disappearance. The news seemed to trigger a depth-charge.

She whirled like a leopardess, the plate she was holding smashing in the sink.

'Are you completely out of your mind?' she shouted. 'Don't you realise that these people are dangerous?'

The outburst took him by surprise and left him momentarily speechless.

She stared at him, tears of anger in her eyes. 'What are you trying to do to us?'

He did his best to placate her. 'I'm helping Patrick, come on, now!'

'Helping Patrick!' she parroted. 'And just what the hell are you doing for me? You're my husband, for God's sake! How do you think I feel?'

'You've made that pretty obvious,' he said. 'Anyway, I've always known how you felt. You were under no illusions when we married.'

The blood had returned to her face and her eyes were hostile.

'And what's that supposed to mean?'

He spread his hands, smiling, hoping for peace. 'It means that I can't change the way that I am. No more, no less.'

'I see,' she replied. 'Two men have been killed. Someone comes aboard this boat and attacks you. Another man vanishes into thin air and you think that's normal. You don't even *think* like other people! You're insane.'

What happened next was misunderstood by both of them, his own quick movement to take her in his arms, her instinctive reaction to protect herself from what she imagined to be a blow. Her open palm had landed flush on the side of his head, shocking him into instant awareness. He felt his head and looked at his hand in astonishment. Then he grabbed her by the shoulders and pinned her against the wall. He heard the voice of a stranger, cold and warning.

'I've never hit a woman in my life, nor have I ever been hit by one. You'd better make sure it's the last time.'

He released her almost contemptuously, his voice still unsteady.

'Lock all the doors and windows. I won't be sleeping here tonight.'

He heard her call as he walked along the deck, knowing that she would only call once and not come running after him. He sat in the car for almost an hour until the lights on the boat were extinguished.

Cooney

He made his way to the hall in his pyjamas. Teresa had already left for work. The only piece of mail was for his sister, a card addressed from Pointe au Baril, Ontario. Written on the back were the words *A moose is bigger than a horse and weighs more than a thousand pounds! Robert Wilson S.J.* He threw the card on the kitchen table and poured himself a bowl of cereal.

He had shaved and finished dressing when the telephone rang. The stranger's voice had an upper-class accent.

'This is Paul Zeller, Mr Dragoti's nephew. I want you to come here now. You know the address.'

Cooney glanced across at the clock. It was half-past eight.

'I'm just leaving for work.'

'This is more important than work,' said the voice. 'I'll be waiting.'

Cooney swallowed the last of his Diludin capsules. His source of supply was a chemist with an undisclosed criminal record. The man was grateful for Cooney's silence.

It was still raining when Cooney reached Campden Hill. He walked around the corner to the exclusive block. Dragoti's nephew was waiting in the doorway of his flat, a handsome man a couple of years younger than Cooney. He was dressed in herringbone tweed slacks and a fawn rollneck sweater. He showed Cooney into the expensively furnished room.

A coffee-percolator bubbled on a glass side-table. The curtains were still closed.

'Sugar and cream?' asked Zeller. There was a hint of arrogance in the way he stood, chin lifted, smiling.

'Sugar,' said Cooney. He knew more about the other man than Zeller supposed. He knew about the cousin in Amsterdam for example, the one Zeller visited, the one who had set this thing up.

The cups were like eggshells. Cooney balanced his on the arm of the chair he was sitting in.

'You want to know why I asked you to come here?' said Zeller.

'I want to know why you called me at home,' said Cooney.

'Why, do you think that your line's bugged?'

'I know that it isn't,' said Cooney. 'It's the principle. I deal with your uncle, not you.'

Zeller perched on the end of the sofa. The cologne he wore was distinctive.

'Let's talk about my uncle,' he said. 'To begin with he's more like a father to me. If you can understand that it'll probably help you with the rest of what I'm going to say.' The smile, the cool hazel eyes, gave him the look of a young Alain Delon. In anyone else it would have been supercilious.

Cooney watched him cautiously.

'My uncle and I have no secrets,' said Zeller. 'I know everything. He's sixty-four years old and a sick man. I don't propose to sit still and watch him get ripped-off. Let's play a game. Suppose you'd staged this whole thing with Slade. How would you have played it?'

94

Cooney smiled to show that he too appreciated a joke. The speed he had taken controlled his composure.

'I wouldn't be sitting here in the first place.'

Zeller moved his head appreciatively. His dark hair rolled over his sweater collar.

'That's a point. But you could be bluffing. Don't get me wrong. This is all supposition. The way I see it you'd have to get rid of Slade. The man was an embarrassment.'

The coffee was suddenly bitter and unpalatable. 'You've got more imagination than I have,' said Cooney.

Zeller's gesture was gallic. 'Slade would have represented a grave threat to your safety.'

A snail of fear crawled into Cooney's consciousness. 'Before you take this crap any further, is this your uncle talking or you?'

'You can assume that it's both of us,' Zeller answered. 'I happen to have a better command of the language.'

'And the cassette?'

'I've thought about that,' Zeller admitted. 'I reckoned that Slade would be doing what he was told to do. You of course would be somewhere else. You know, where people would remember seeing you.'

Cooney put his coffee-cup back on the table. 'I don't have to sit here and listen to this shit.'

'Relax!' said Zeller, smiling. 'I'll be honest with you. All that's been spinning around in my head since Saturday night. Now someone else has appeared on the scene and I'm having to revise my thinking. What do you know of a man called Raven?'

Cooney ran the name through his head without finding a point of reference. Speed made him sensitive to heat and cold alike and he found the room uncomfortably warm. It was a relief to be able to give a straight answer.

'The name means nothing,' he said.

'It should do,' said Zeller, refilling his coffee-cup. 'He lives on a houseboat on Cheyne Walk, a boat called the *Albatross*.'

Cooney turned his wrist and looked at his watch. 'I'm supposed to be at work.'

'Raven's been round to Rivermead Court asking questions.'

'So?' Cooney searched his pocket for a light.

'The porter is scared and no wonder. First it's the police asking questions, then the lawyer and Raven. Now me. He's left Rivermead Court and he won't be going back. I found him a better job in Scotland.'

Cooney released a thin stream of smoke.

'He told Raven that you'd been to see Guerin,' said Zeller.

'Doesn't mean a thing,' said Cooney. 'I spoke to the porter once and that was months ago.'

Zeller nodded slowly. 'Raven's got a picture of you. The porter identified it.'

'Jesus Christ!' said Cooney. The news both shocked and alarmed him. 'Where did he get my picture from?'

'Yours *and* Slade's,' said Zeller. 'I'll tell you something else I found out. There's a back way into Rivermead Court through the boiler-room. The door's kept locked but I found it no problem. Just a few steps and you're up in the corridor. You can't be seen from the lobby. Whoever killed Guerin must have gone in that way.'

'I wouldn't know,' said Cooney. It was getting to be a problem, maintaining the conversational tone and manner.

'Raven,' said Zeller. 'In the first place he's a close friend of the lawyer. In the second place he's an ex-cop.'

Cooney blinked. The snail of fear that had been torpid stirred again.

'Are you being serious?'

'It's not the sort of thing I'd joke about,' answered Zeller. 'He retired from the force eight years ago. I checked him out with someone. The man's a trouble-maker. A self-appointed crusader. And he happens to have money. It's a dangerous combination.'

'You're damn right.' Cooney spoke from the heart. 'What's he looking for? What's his angle?'

'The same thing that we're looking for, I suspect. My uncle's diamonds. I want you to pay him a visit, Cooney.'

Cooney felt his feet slipping from under him. 'Pay him a visit?'

Zeller nodded encouragingly. 'That's right. You're just the man for the job.'

Zeller, the heat in the room, the news about Raven. Cooney found them all disturbing.

'What are you people trying to do to me?' he demanded.

Zeller released his slow smile. 'I'm trying to get my uncle's property back. You say that you haven't got it and that you don't know who has. OK, on balance I'm inclined to believe you. There's a chance that Raven knows more than we do. That's what I want you to find out.'

'What am I supposed to say to him?' asked Cooney. The idea was growing more alarming by the second.

Zeller passed his hand through his thick hair.

'You're a cop and you know that he's been at Rivermead Court asking questions. That's enough to get your foot in the door.'

'The last thing I want at the moment is to get involved in a murder enquiry,' said Cooney. 'It's the last thing any of us wants.'

Zeller opened the curtains. Rain was still falling outside. He spoke with his back to Cooney, as casually as if he were asking the time.

'Then we'll do it a different way. You'll get a telephone message supposedly from one of your snitches. It'll give you Raven's name and address. You can supply the rest of the thinking.'

Cooney wiped his forehead. He was beginning to sweat, 'Suppose I told you that the whole idea's crazy?'

Zeller raised his shoulders. 'I'd be forced to believe the worst of you. I told you, my uncle's a sick man. I'm looking after him. I'd like to think that you're on my side.'

Their eyes battled and Cooney was the first to break. 'I'll do what I can,' he muttered.

Zeller came to the door with him, wary yet confident. He moved like a duelist on his way to an encounter.

'You'll get your money,' he promised quietly. 'We're honest people. See Raven today. I've got a feeling about him. I think he'll lead us where we want to go.'

He closed the door quietly, leaving Cooney alone in the lobby. It was a quick drive to Paddington. Things had to be done in their order of precedence. The continual downpour made the street even shabbier. A bell tinkled as Cooney opened the door of the chemist's. A bald man was serving a woman. He glanced at Cooney warningly. Cooney waited. It was a one-man business selling cut-price goods to the poor. Elixirs for the lungs and bowels; baskets of bargain toiletries; cheap scent and corn-plasters. Cooney waited until the woman had left and he was alone with the chemist.

'You can fill me up this time, Harry,' he said. 'Give me the box.'

The Diludin came in boxes containing twenty bottles. There were twenty capsules in each small bottle.

The chemist shook his head. 'I can't do that, Cooney. Come on, be reasonable. If the man checks my book I'm in trouble. You know that!'

'So fake it, said Cooney. 'You've been doing it all your life.' He placed a ten pound note on the counter.

The chemist unlocked a cupboard and emptied the box into a plastic bag.

'You can keep the change,' said Cooney, putting the bag in the pocket of his trenchcoat.

The man let his breath go. 'When am I going to get you off my bleeding back?'

'As of this moment,' said Cooney. He reached across the counter and tapped the other man's shoulder. 'So long, Harry. No hard feelings.'

He put the bag of Diludin in the boot, keeping one bottle loose in his pocket. Things were moving faster than he had anticipated and not always in the right direction. He had to maintain control.

Birley's car was outside the police station, the driver at the wheel. Cooney parked in the space reserved for unit officers and walked up the steps. The hall had the familiar smell of bacon sandwiches. The duty sergeant passed a piece of paper across the desk. Cooney read it.

TIMED 09 58.

MALE VOICE SPEAKING FROM A PUBLIC
CALL-BOX.

This message is for Detective Sergeant Cooney.
The name and address he wants is John Raven,
Houseboat Albatross, Chelsea Embankment.

The desk sergeant winked, looking up at the clock
on the wall.

'Got to hand it to you, Cooney. You're a mover.
Commander Birley'd like to see you if you'd be good
enough to step along to his room.'

Cooney just smiled at him. He collected the list he
had made on the previous day, a compendium of
arrests made by Slade and him, the names of the
offenders concerned and the disposition of the
charges. The list for the previous year contained the
essential details of two hundred charges. One hundred and thirty-two had resulted in convictions. It
was the highest striking rate of any team on the
Squad.

He knocked on Birley's door and entered. Birley
removed the pipe from his mouth and emitted a
cloud of Gold Block tobacco smoke. The room reeked
of it. Cooney found himself a lot surer here than he
had been in Zeller's apartment.

He dropped into the chair that was placed for him.
'I'm sorry I'm late, sir. I had someone to see.'

He pushed the message across the desk.

'I saw it,' said Birley.

'One of my informants,' said Cooney. 'He claims
there's a tie-in with Slade.'

Birley's nod confirmed the unwritten law. An
informer was the property of the officer concerned. A

rosebud sprouted in Birley's lapel.

'Is this man reliable?'

Cooney looked confident. 'He always has been.'

'I've got a special reason for asking,' said Birley. 'Does the name Raven mean anything to you?'

Cooney nodded. 'I think so, sir, yes. If it's the same man. Dave and I were sitting in the car just off Sloane Square. This man came out of a house nearby. Dave was out of the car in a flash. The pair of them stood there talking. When Dave came back I asked who the other guy was. Just someone he knew, he said. He didn't mention a name and I didn't ask. But I got to thinking last night and made some enquiries. What you just read is the answer.'

Birley knocked the bowl of his pipe into the ashtray, savouring the name.

'John Raven. I'll tell you about Mr Raven, sergeant. He served under me on the Drugs Squad. He was a good cop with one major defect. He made his own rules and that got him into trouble. So much trouble, in fact, that he had to resign. Since then he's been making a thorough nuisance of himself, carrying on a one-man campaign against the force. I won't say that he hasn't been right on occasions. He's opened some barrels of rotten fish. It's the way that he's done it that's wrong. He's a wrecker, Cooney. The idea that he's even remotely involved with Slade worries me a great deal.'

'Do you mind if I smoke?' asked Cooney. Things were looking good again.

'Go ahead,' Birley answered. 'You'd be a lot better off with a pipe, but that's your business. No, Raven's just about the last person in the world we want on the scene at this moment.' He rattled his fingernails on the desk-top.

Cooney exhaled. 'You want me to drop this line of enquiry, is that it?'

'No,' Birley said quickly. 'That's not what I had in mind. Rutherford's doing the post mortem on Thursday, right. I don't have to tell you that we're in a tricky situation as far as the media are concerned. We can't afford any leaks until we're on top of this thing. No, I want you to see Mr Raven. Just watch your step. The man is no fool.'

Cooney affected to give it some thought. 'Couldn't I say that Slade gave me his name and go from there? I could invent some sort of message.'

'And what do you say about Slade?'

'That's the difficulty,' Cooney answered. 'Whenever I've been asked I refer them to you.'

Birley left the desk to pace. He swung round halfway to the window.

'Slade's been posted on special assignment to Belfast. That won't hold water for too long.' He opened a drawer and pulled out a gold watch and strap. 'Ever see this before?'

Cooney recognised it instantly. It had been on Guerin's bedroom table. Slade must have taken it.

Cooney offered his ingenuous smile. 'It's a little out of my price range, sir.'

'Mine as well.' Birley returned the watch to the drawer. 'We're talking about a watch I'm told is worth eighteen hundred pounds or more, a Patek Phillippe. The Swiss Centre says that it should be easy to trace. They're working on it now.'

Cooney strove for the casual look, crossing one leg over the other and leaning forward.

'Where did it come from, sir?'

'You may well ask,' Birley answered. 'Someone suggested a second look at Slade's car. They found the watch jammed under the accelerator. I've got a feeling it could be important.'

Cooney was starting to sweat again. If the watch was traced back to Guerin, the link between him and Slade would be established. He did his best to keep his voice normal.

'Do we know anything more about the diamond?'

Birley continued to walk, six paces left, turn, six paces right.

'Not a lot, no, sergeant. The man we use in Hatton Garden says that it's certainly South African and probably cut and polished in Europe. There's an outside chance that could have been done in Israel. All of which doesn't take us far. It wasn't stolen. It's not on any of the lists.'

Cooney spread his hands. 'I'm running out of ideas.'

Birley came to a halt. 'I've got a feeling that Raven might be the breakthrough we need. But you're going to have to tread delicately. Don't be aggressive whatever you do. That line won't work. Remember that Raven does have connections. Not only that, he's prepared to use them. Feel your way. I'll leave that to you. But for Christ's sake be careful.'

'Don't worry, sir,' Cooney assured him. 'I've got a special interest in Mr Raven. I don't like being made a fool of.'

Birley had the watch out again, looking at it. 'If you need any help you come straight through to me. Not a word of anything that's said in this room to anyone. Understood?'

Cooney raised his eyes. 'How about C.R. Eleven?'

'*Nobody*,' said Birley. 'This is between you and me for the moment. Report to me the moment you've seen Raven. And you can take that list of arrests away with you. Raven's our priority.'

'I've got the picture, sir.'

A sudden look of curiosity spread over Birley's face. 'Where do you get your clothes?'

Cooney ventured a modest smile. 'January sales, most of them, sir.'

'January sales, eh? I'll have to remember that. I like to see a man who's well turned-out.'

Cooney was sure of one thing now. He had Birley eating out of his hand. Cooney sat in the car, reflecting that he himself was touched with magic. Admittedly there had been a nasty moment with Zeller. All that supposition stuff had come dangerously close to the truth. But Zeller's suspicions appeared to have been switched to Raven. Fostering this was the obvious ploy. The idea of Raven and Slade as partners was a good one. Guerin, Raven and Slade even better.

Cooney explored the thought. Slade kills Guerin then Raven kills Slade leaving Raven with the loot. The more Cooney dwelt upon it, the stronger his conviction became that Dragoti would buy the notion. Anyone chasing a million-and-a-quarter pounds is prone to believe the worst of everyone.

Cooney took a cursory glance in the mirror as he started the Jaguar. He was reasonably sure that he was not being tailed but too much was at stake to be complacent. He ate in a Jewish restaurant, bean-and-barley soup, fried fish with horseradish. He pocketed a handful of toothpicks and strolled back along Great Windmill Street. Once in the car, he switched on the police radio. Coded signals crackled in the speakers. None of what was said applied to him. He parked off Fulham Road and walked three hundred yards to the studios. There was no-one else in the house. The traffic outside his windows offered the occasional blare of a car-horn. He swallowed a couple of Diludin capsules. There was reason now to ration himself. Not that he was addicted. Speed kept his head together under pressure. He unwrapped one of the papers of diamonds.

The loose stones were slightly greasy to the touch yet at the same time angled and hard. He filled his palms with the packages. There was something nerve-tingling about sitting in a glorified flophouse holding a fortune in his hands. He had a sense of being unique in a city of eight million people, above all ordinary standards. He replaced the diamonds in the flight-bag with his passport and ticket. The envelope in the bag contained twelve hundred pounds, all he needed to reach his destination. Once there he had the addresses he wanted. All he required was a few hours' start. After that no-one could touch him.

He turned the key in the cupboard. The thought that he had killed two men for what was inside occasioned neither fear nor remorse. As the man said, after the first the rest don't count. He'd blown Guerin's head asunder without compunction and had no remorse about Slade. The strongest deterrent to crime was the fear of getting caught.

He left the Jaguar where it was and walked down to the Embankment. He leaned over the parapet. Twenty boats floated below on the river. They were of all shapes and sizes. Barges, narrow and wide, a couple of tenders, a Maidenhead houseboat, home-built craft and one smart sailing-boat. A network of planks and ropes fastened the flotilla together. It seemed that if one boat foundered the rest must surely follow.

Cooney descended the steps to a small jetty. A door festooned with barbed-wire blocked the way to the gangway beyond. Craning, Cooney could see the wide-beamed black barge. He spoke into the entryphone and a woman's voice answered.

He used his respectful manner. 'Detective Sergeant Cooney. Ma'am.'

The hesitation was brief. 'Is it about my husband?'

'Yes, it is,' said Cooney.

The door clicked open. He hung onto the guide-rope, the planks shifting under his feet. Flowers were growing in tubs on the deck. The woman standing in the door of the superstructure was in her middle thirties, long legged in jeans and sweater. Her eyes were etched with anxiety, her hair the colour of peaty water.

'Come in,' she said quickly, extending her hand for his coat.

It was a long room with windows built into its contours. Cooney's practised inspection picked out the Bang and Olufsen stereo-system, the silver frames and cigarette boxes, some kind of abstract painting. There were shelves crammed with records and tapes and a bronze figure of a rearing stallion. The carpet they were standing on was worn and darned, the colours faded.

The woman gestured nervously. 'I'm sorry. I'm Kirstie Raven. Do please sit down.'

'Is there any chance of talking to your husband?' asked Cooney.

It took no more than seconds then the words came with a rush.

'I thought that was why you were here. There's not a lot of sense pussyfooting around. The truth is that my husband and I had a fight last night, one of the nastier kind with both of us losing our tempers. He's a difficult man to deal with at times. I suppose we're both difficult. Anyway, he stormed off the boat at one o'clock this morning and that's the last I saw of him.'

He gave her his man-of-the-world smile. 'Give him a little time, Mrs Raven. These things do happen. We see a lot of it.'

She was obviously distraught and disposed to talk. 'I've called all our friends and the Royal Automobile Club. He's a member and I thought that he might have spent the night there but nobody's seen him. I'm worried, Mr Cooney.'

'I'm sure there's no need to be.' He leaned back comfortably. 'It's only been a matter of a few hours.'

Her eyes widened perceptibly. 'But this isn't like him at all. And he's taken his car. You know what people are like when they're upset. They take chances. He could have been in an accident.'

'I doubt it,' he said. 'He probably had too much to drink and booked into some hotel. Give him a little more time, Mrs Raven. He'll be back with a bunch of flowers, you'll see.'

It was plain that the idea had no appeal to her. 'You don't know my husband,' she said. 'He rarely gets drunk and he certainly won't buy me flowers. He'll be far too sure that he's in the right.'

The speed was still working and Cooney saw everything clearly. He was indeed touched with magic. A new twist in his plot had occurred to him. One that would further involve the missing Raven.

He leaned back in his chair. 'I shouldn't be really talking to you, Mrs Raven, but I'll take a chance. This isn't supposed to be an official visit. I'm here as a friend.'

A pulse beat in her throat as she stared at her

fingers. It took her a while to form her question.

'He's not in some kind of trouble, is he?'

He looked at her frankly. 'I'm afraid he could be, Mrs Raven.'

Her eyes sought his face. 'Can you tell me what it is, please?'

'I've never met your husband,' he said. 'But I know a lot about him. He's created a lot of problems since he left the force. Don't get me wrong! This is nothing personal. But he does get involved with things that are none of his business. And he's doing that at this moment. That's why I'm here. I want to stop him before it's too late.'

She was twisting her rings again, her face stressed by new concern.

He moved into low-key sincerity, the pose that had made him the star of the interview room.

'Let me ask you a question. Do you know the name Slade?'

Her eyes flickered briefly. It was enough.

'I thought so,' he said. 'Look Mrs Raven, I'm here because I'd hoped to talk some sense to your husband. He's been lucky in the past. This time he's going to get burned.' He glanced through the window. Some freak with a green beard and an enormous dog was standing on the end of the neighbouring gangway.

She nibbled her lower lip, studying him. 'How do I know that you're really a policeman?'

He showed her his warrant card. 'Tell your husband that I won't be back, Mrs Raven. In fact I was never here. He'll understand.'

The man called from the gangway. She was up like a flash, running along the deck. Cooney moved to the desk. The second drawer he opened was full of loose photographs. Most of them featured the man who stared out from the silver frame. Cooney selected a colour print of Raven at the wheel of a sailing boat. Spray partly obscured his body and arms but his face was plainly recognisable. The words *See what you're missing!* were scrawled across the photograph. Cooney slipped it into his blazer pocket and was back in his seat before she left the gangway.

She opened the door, her face dejected. 'That was our neighbour. I asked him to make some calls. No luck, I'm afraid.'

He gave her the follow-up treatment, the friendly voice as the cell-door closed on a capture.

'He'll be back shortly and give him the message. "All people want is what belongs to them."'

He took his coat from where it was hanging. 'Goodbye, Mrs Raven, it's been nice meeting you.'

She nodded abstractedly, her mind was on something else. 'What was that name again, the one you mentioned?'

'Slade,' he said. 'Goodbye, Mrs Raven.'

He hurried back to the car and took a long look at the picture he'd taken. He used the nearest call box and rang Beryl Slade.

'It's me, Cooney,' he said.

The news brought an immediate rasp to her voice. 'I might have guessed. What the hell do you want?'

He clicked his tongue. 'That's no way to talk to a man who's about to make your fortune. I've got a proposition for you. It could be worth a great deal of money.'

'You know what to do with it,' she answered. 'Any proposition coming from you is bound to be dodgy. And you can stop sending those creeps to see me.'

'What creeps?' he said. 'I don't know what you're

talking about. Does a hundred grand interest you?'

Her tone changed decisively. 'How do you mean?'

He brought the mouthpiece closer. 'I can't say too much on the phone, but your ex was sitting on a fortune when he copped it. I've got a lot of the bits and pieces but I need your help to complete. I'm talking about the thing that was found on him. Do you understand what I mean?'

He could hear her brain ticking. 'I understand,' she said in a low voice.

'Good,' he said. 'Can I see you this evening? It's better if I come to you.'

'What sort of time did you have in mind? There's a friend coming round about half-past six. I can't very well put her off. Can we make it tomorrow?'

'Then early,' he said. 'I'll be there at nine. There's a lot to talk about.'

He replaced the phone as though undue noise would betray his intention. He paid a visit to a hardware shop where he bought a tin of paint and shoplifted a hammer. He spent the next couple of hours driving round aimlessly. Once it was dark he headed for Streatham.

He did the last couple of hundred yards on foot. The rain had slackened, lifted on the wind that separated the last leaves from the trees. He kept to the unlit stretches of road, his footsteps inaudible. As often as he heard someone coming, he hid until danger had passed.

The front of Slade's house was in darkness. Cooney flitted across the wet grass. A yale-type lock secured the side-gate. Cooney opened it with a plastic credit card. Brick walls concealed him as far as the shrubbery. He sheltered under a dripping laburnum tree. A light showed behind closed curtains on the second floor. Music was playing. The kitchen was immediately below the bedroom. Cooney picked up a stone and tossed it at the roof. He heard it rattle down the tiles and strike the garbage-can. The noise evoked no reaction from upstairs. His second attempt brought movement at the curtains. Beryl Slade looked down from the window and closed the curtains again. His third throw moved her downstairs. A light came on in the kitchen. Cooney put his back against the wall as the door opened. The garden was briefly illuminated. The shadow lengthened as Bery Slade took a tentative step forward, peering into the dank shrubbery. Cooney's gloved hand found the hammer handle. He was quickly behind her, swinging, the whole of his hundred and sixty pounds behind the blow. The impact jarred his arm so that the hammer-head turned. Her hands went up to the back of her head and she staggered sideways, reeling back into the kitchen. He hit her a second time, blotting out the look of recognition that accused him. Blood sprang from the shattered bone, spattering the front of his clothing. He cut the lights and stood in the darkness breathing heavily. It was the only sound that he heard. There was none from the body lying beside him. He left Beryl Slade where she was and ran upstairs to the bathroom. He stared at himself in the mirror. The front of his shirt and his blazer were badly stained. He wiped the worst from his blazer with a face flannel. There was nothing he could do about the shirt. He flushed the flannel down the lavatory and checked his shoes. The soles were clean.

Slade's bedroom was at the end of the short corridor. A light showed the unmade bed. The flannel pyjamas were on the floor as Slade had left them. Cooney exchanged his shirt for one that he found in a drawer and bundled his own into his pocket. His Burberry had been partly open and was unsoiled. A cardboard file on the dressing-table contained Slade's personal papers. Passport, birth and marriage certificates, a life-insurance policy. Cooney tucked the stolen picture in among the other papers. He tiptoed down the stairs. The radio was still playing in Beryl Slade's bedroom. He snapped the kitchen light on and off. There was no need for a second look. He drew himself water from the sink, avoiding the blood on the floor. His heart was beating faster. Nothing had changed in the house but the body beside him.

He opened a crack in the front door and then wider as his senses assured him of safety. He walked away quickly, restraining himself from running. Rain blew on the wind in his face. There was nobody on the street. Back in the car, he reached for the Diludin. The rush took him quickly. He headed the Jaguar over the hill and down towards Crystal Palace. The houses were drab and closed. Only the lights showed that people lived there. He stopped by a drain, poked his bloodstained shirt through the grating and dropped the hammer and his gloves after it.

He made his way back through the suburbs. Coded announcements were beginning to come over the police band. *Report female killed in Streatham.* Replies showed that cars were responding. Cooney listened as he drove, his control restored. Beryl Slade's friend had been punctual. The seeds had been sown. The supposed meeting between Slade and Raven. Raven's picture among Slade's papers. The fruit could hardly be denied.

Cooney called Zeller from a pub in Kensington. 'I've been on the boat. Raven wasn't there. His wife claims that she doesn't know where he is. She says that they quarrelled last night and he walked off the boat.'

The other man's voice was bitter. 'My uncle had a coronary this morning. He's in intensive care at Charing Cross Hospital.'

Cooney's first feeling was one of relief. 'I'm sorry,' he said.

'You'd better be,' Zeller replied. 'I'm holding you responsible.'

Cooney turned his back on a man who was standing nearby. 'Now look,' he said to Zeller. 'We've been through all this. I'm doing my best and we've still got chances. If Raven's got the diamonds I'll give you my word that he's not going anywhere.'

'I don't want your word,' answered Zeller. 'Your word's not worth shit.'

'I'll find him,' said Cooney.

'You do that,' said Zeller. 'My uncle may be in hospital but I'm still around. And you'd better believe I mean business!'

'I'll call you tomorrow morning. By then I'll have news.'

The red light on the dashboard was blinking when Cooney reached the car. The operator's voice was curt.

'Where the hell have you been?'

'Eating,' said Cooney.

'I've got Commander Birley on the line.'

Cooney took a deep breath, composing himself against the storm that must surely break.

Birley sounded agitated. 'Where are you, sergeant?'

Cooney gave his position.

'Drop everything and get back to Holloway. I mean

now.'

Cooney stowed the radiophone under the dash. There was no flak, no problem. Just another shout for help to the man who could be relied upon.

Raven

When Raven left the cinema the rain had slackened. He had dozed through the film, tired after a night spent in a strange bed. He had slept in the Chelsea Arts Club. He pointed the Saab west along Fulham Road. He parked near the junction with Sydney Street. *Chez Marius* was tucked away in a cul-de-sac. He pushed through the dusty velvet curtains. This was the only genuine Provençal restaurant in London. There were no lobster-pots or fishing-nets draped on the walls, no Spanish waiters tricked-out in tight Camargue pants. The paintwork was white ripple and the floor was laid with straw matting. Good food was served on earthenware plates and the wine was regional.

Raven hung his mac on the bamboo stand and straightened his hair with his fingers. He had borrowed a razor but had slept in the check-shirt and it looked like it. Madame Bialgue took his hand. She was a large woman with massive breasts. She was dressed entirely in black and wore her dark-brown hair in a bun on her neck, giving the impression of a Roman matron. Her smile, like everything else about her, generated warmth and friendliness. With Kirstie and Raven she always spoke French.

'Monsieur Raven, alone? And where is Madame?'

'She's in Paris,' he lied. He glanced round the room. All twelve tables were occupied.

'No problem,' his hostess said quickly. She signalled to her daughter and the two women pulled a table from behind a door and placed it close to the window. The restaurant was run by the family. Marius Bialgue and his son-in-law worked in the kitchen. His wife and daughter served the food. Christine Cazenove was like her father, lean and slightly wild-eyed. She stayed to take Raven's order, pencil poised in readiness, offering the mild flirtation that she always enjoyed with Raven.

'Madame is not very serious, leaving you alone in London.'

'She knows that your husband is a jealous man,' he replied. The black olives were plump, he spat the stones into his palm and deposited them in the ashtray. She leaned over his shoulder, releasing the provocative scent of *Jolie Madame*, graceful in a black skirt and ivory-lace blouse. He ordered hare paté, hot garlic bread and bouillabaisse and a well-chilled rosé to go with it. She traced the movements of her pencil with the tip of her tongue and looked down, smiling.

'An apéritif to start with?'

'Just the wine,' he said, 'thank you.'

She held a degree in languages from the Sorbonne, was married to an assistant-chef and would have ordered her life in no other way. The clientele was mostly French, business people and members of the faculty at the nearby Lycée. The Bialgues ran the place like a club. There was a warm welcome extended to those who were favoured, gallic exclusion for those who were not. Raven dawdled over his food. Christine brought him a Marc de Champagne with the compliments of the house. He smoked a cigarette, waiting for the coffee to drip through the filter. It was on his mind to call Kirstie, to tell her he was on his way. Their quarrel the previous night had left him deeply disturbed. And now it was time to go home. He paid his bill, accepting a box of nougat that Kirstie always enjoyed. It was a few minutes after ten o'clock. The pubs and restaurants along King's Road were still busy in spite of the weather. He was glad that he hadn't called Kirstie. It was better just to arrive. No apologies, no explanations, just hold one another tight.

He brought the radio to life. A Fats Waller programme was playing on Paris-Inter. Raven hummed along with the melody, waiting for the signals to change. He was first away, followed by the wail of a police siren. Lights flashed in the rear-view mirror. He stamped on the brakes and pulled to the left. The police car shot past and swung over, forcing the Saab to the kerb. A ginger-haired plain clothes-man jumped out and rapped on Raven's window.

'Police! Out!'

Two more plain clothes-men closed in. The moment Raven's feet touched ground his arms were pinned from behind, his legs kicked apart. Someone rammed his head forward against the side of the car. Hands searched his pockets and felt down his body.

Raven turned slowly, rain running down his neck. The ginger-haired man offered a quick glimpse of a warrant card. His name was Detective Sergeant Pannel. One of the other men slipped behind the wheel of the Saab.

'What's all this about?' Raven demanded, rebuttoning his mackinaw.

Pannel's old blue coat no longer shed rain. After the first display of violence his manner was civil.

'Do you mind getting in the squad car, sir?'

Raven stood his ground. 'Not before you tell me what this is about.'

Pannel took Raven's arm. 'Come on, you know the game better than I do. Don't make things awkward.'

They walked towards the waiting vehicle. The lights on Battersea Bridge showed no more than a couple of hundred yards away. Raven was almost within shouting distance of home. He sat in the back of the squad car, locked in by Pannel and one of the other men. The two vehicles performed an illegal u-turn and shot off in the direction of Lucan Place. They stopped in front of Chelsea Police Station. The plain clothes-men escorted him up the steps. He knew the premises of old. The charge room was still the same, the walls decorated with posters of wanted men, the calendar supplied by the firm of handcuff-makers. The station sergeant was a placid-looking man with an array of pens and pencils worn in his shirt pocket.

He looked from Raven to his captors. 'What's this, then?'

Pannel leaned across and whispered in the sergeant's ear. The sergeant nodded amiably at Raven.

'Not carrying any offensive weapons or explosives, are you, sir?'

'He's clean,' said Pannel. 'Is anyone here yet?'

'They're on their way,' said the sergeant, his eye on the clock on the wall. It was five minutes past eleven. Pannel checked the time with his watch.

'Am I under arrest?' he said to the sergeant.

The sergeant shook his head. 'No, sir. You're either a volunteer helping the police with their enquiries or you're detained while we verify your particulars. You take your pick.'

The other two men appreciated the sally and grinned. Raven pulled a cigarette from the packet. No-one attempted to stop him lighting it. He leaned against the wall and blew smoke at the street.

'I'd like to make a phone call.'

Pannel made a sound of annoyance. 'You know, I guessed you were going to say that! All our lines are engaged at the moment. Let's try again later. This way, please.'

Raven followed Pannel up the stairs. He knew every inch of the building from the basement garage to the Matron's and W.P.C.'s quarters on the top floor. Pannel stopped at the second storey and jerked his head left. The room was at the front, overlooking Lucan Place.

'You'll be comfortable here,' said Pannel. He winked and shut the door behind him.

Raven took stock. The door had no handle on the inside and the windows were barred. He must have put hundreds of men in rooms like this in his time, but the view was different on this occasion. There was a table with a formica top, three plain deal chairs and an empty water carafe. The scars of an ancient gouging had withstood the fresh coats of paint and Raven could read the legend:

ADJUST YOUR STORY – YOU ARE AMONG DISBELIEVERS

Raven glanced down through the rain-spotted window. The glow from the police station entrance took in the Saab parked outside. He put his ear against the door. A telephone was ringing unanswered somewhere. His nose detected coffee brewing. When he looked at his watch again it was half-past eleven. He sat down on a chair. At least they had left him his lighter and cigarettes. He tried to work out what had hit him. He was in the clear as far as his visit to Rivermead Court went. He had gone there with Patrick. It had to be something of greater importance. He straightened his back, hit by the obvious. *The porter, of course*! He could well be in another room, talking his head off. But about what? The man who had been on the boat, Mystery X? One thing was for sure. Whatever Lambert was confiding was linked to Guerin's murder.

The door opened without prior warning. Two men came in. The one in front was in his fifties with a quick step and direct gaze. His hair was white and he wore a handknitted cardigan under his tweed jacket. He had aged but Raven remembered him well.

'It's been a long time,' said Raven.

Birley's smile came and went. 'Seventeen years?'

'Something like that,' said Raven.

'This is Detective Sergeant Cooney,' said Birley.

The two men nodded at one another. Cooney's long blond hair hung from a side parting. His eyes were those of a wolf. He was bigger than his picture suggested.

Birley indicated the chairs. 'We might as well sit while we're waiting.'

They sat facing one another, Birley tapping his teeth with the stem of his pipe. Cooney stood off to one side.

'Do you know why you're here?' asked Birley.

Raven shook his head. 'Tell me.'

'Let's not play games,' said the Commander. 'I'm trying to conduct this thing in a civilised manner.'

The steam radiator clanked suddenly. Raven waited for the noise to subside.

'I'm not playing games,' he said quietly. 'I've been pulled out of my car, body-searched in the pouring rain and told that I can't make a phone call. Is that what you mean by a civilised manner?'

Birley used his pipe-stem as a pointer. 'You could have been down in the cells, you know. That's where the Murder Squad would have had you.'

'*Murder Squad?*' Raven repeated. 'What the hell are you talking about?'

Birley swung himself sideways like an old-fashioned preacher, propelling his shoulder forward.

'I'm going to ask you one question, John. It's up to you whether or not you answer it. Do you know a Detective Inspector Slade?'

Raven held up his hand. 'Shouldn't you be cautioning me?'

'You're cautioned,' said Birley. 'Do you know Slade or not?'

'You mean *did* I know him, no.'

'Then you know that he's dead?'

'His wife told me.'

'What were you doing talking to his wife?'

'Asking where Slade was. I wanted to ask him a personal question.'

'That's bullshit,' said Cooney. 'You were talking to him near Sloane Square, back in the summer. I saw you myself.'

Raven looked at Birley. 'Will you please get this clown out of here?'

Birley paid no attention. 'Slade's wife tells a different story. She says that you and Slade were friends, that you went to their house on several occasions.'

'I was there once.' Raven found a shred of tobacco on his lip and discarded it.

The Commander wagged his head sorrowfully. 'You used to be a good cop. It was a pity you left us.'

Raven's smile was wry. 'The way I remember things I didn't have much choice.'

'You made sure of that,' said Birley. 'One thing's very clear to me since then. You have no loyalty left. I'm talking about loyalty to the force.'

Raven met his challenge directly. 'Is there any expected?'

'There's one thing I want you to understand,' said Birley. 'I've got a good bunch of men working with me. I'm not going to let them suffer for the sake of someone else. Do I make myself clear?'

A knock at the door saved Raven the trouble of answering. The ginger-haired plain clothes-man pushed his head in.

'It's Mr O'Callaghan, sir.'

Raven sprang to his feet, not understanding how his friend had arrived, but grateful for his presence.

'Thank Christ you're here! I don't know the hell what's going on!'

Birley had a brief word with Cooney who left the room. The Commander, grey, correct and courteous, introduced himself to the lawyer.

'My name is Birley, Mr O'Callaghan. Please sit down.'

O'Callaghan took Cooney's chair. His eyes were puffy and he was wearing a grey tweed overcoat with a green velvet collar. He loosened the scarf at his neck, giving a glimpse of his pyjama jacket.

'You'll have to excuse me,' he said with the diffidence he always displayed rather than aggression. 'I was in bed.'

Birley nodded as a man does, called by duty. 'I'd like to clarify your client's position.'

Raven gave him no chance to elaborate. 'I'm helping them with their enquiries, Patrick. My feet haven't touched the ground.'

Birley leaned forward, concentrating on the lawyer. 'I think that we should talk things over calmly, Mr O'Callaghan.'

Raven found his exclusion from the conversation annoying and his manner showed it.

'They stopped me in the middle of Beaufort Street, Patrick. Like some kind of gangster movie!'

Birley kept talking. 'I give you my word, Mr O'Callaghan. Whatever is said in this room goes no further. I know your reputation. That's why I asked you to come here. We're both on the same side of the fence.'

It was impossible for Raven to restrain himself. This was too much.

'You must be joking!' he said. 'On the same side of the fence? Where does that leave me when you've finished your place-setting?'

O'Callaghan waved him down. 'I'm not quite sure that I'm with you, Commander. Your job's the detection of crime. I defend the people you arrest.'

Birley hung one knee over another. 'But we understand one another. No charge has been brought against Mr Raven.'

'I've been here for almost two hours,' said Raven. 'Look at the door! There's no handle.'

Birley waited patiently for silence. 'I'll be frank with you, Mr O'Callaghan. A man called Slade was killed a few days ago, a detective inspector. The circumstances of his death don't really matter for the moment. He was a crook and that *does* matter. A crooked cop is ten times worse than your ordinary villain. He betrays his comrades as well as the public he's supposed to serve.'

Raven shook his head. It seemed that he was forgotten. 'He'll get around to me in a moment,' he said.

But Birley was in full flow. 'There's some testimony that Mr Raven knew Slade. That he went to Slade's house on several occasions.'

'Not true,' Raven protested. 'I went there once.'

'A photograph of your client was found there,' said Birley.

Raven closed his eyes and blew hard. 'I know nothing about a photograph,' he said looking at O'Callaghan.

O'Callaghan looked at the end of his cigarette. 'What testimony are you relying upon, Commander?'

'Mrs Slade's.'

'In that case,' said the lawyer, 'I assume that we'll have the opportunity of challenging it?'

'Unfortunately, no,' Birley responded. There was an element of smugness in his response. 'Somebody killed her tonight.'

Raven jumped to his feet. 'What are they trying to do to me, Patrick?'

O'Callaghan was at his most formal. 'Is my client under suspicion of murder, Commander?'

Birley withstood the onslaught calmly. 'Let's be realistic here. A woman's been savagely beaten to death. Mr Raven's photograph was found in the house. One of my officers states that he saw Mr Raven with Slade. It's possible that he could be mistaken.'

'Or lying!' said Raven.

'You haven't answered my question, Commander.' The lawyer repeated it. 'Is John suspected of murder?'

'Let's put it this way,' said Birley. 'The officer in charge of the investigation would like to know where Mr Raven was between six and seven this evening.'

O'Callaghan sniffed hard and found his handkerchief. 'Suppose I advise him to answer no more questions?'

Commander Birley spread his hands.

'Don't worry,' Raven said quickly. His confidence faded as he searched his pockets uselessly for the cinema-stub. He lit another cigarette.

'I was in the ABC cinema in Fulham Road. The film I saw was a re-run of *Klute*. I was first in. The man who sold me the ticket would remember. When the film finished I had a meal in a restaurant off Fulham Road, *Chez Marius*. You people know the rest. I was on my way home when you grabbed me.'

Birley had his pen out. 'How do you spell the name of that restaurant?' He scribbled on a piece of paper. 'You'll appreciate that this has to be checked.'

'Check away,' said Raven.

Birley excused himself, leaving the other two men alone. Raven felt under the table and radiator. There was no sign that the room was bugged. He came close to the lawyer.

'Why hasn't anyone mentioned Guerin?'

O'Callaghan put his finger against his lips. A quarter of an hour passed. The door was opened again. A Pakistani looked in from the corridor. Birley and Cooney were behind him. The ticket-seller stared at Raven as he might have done at a cobra. His voice shook with nervousness.

'Oh yes!' He nodded repeatedly. 'No doubt at all! This gentleman was in the cinema this evening.'

'See he gets back where he wants to go,' said Birley. He watched from the window as the police car drove off.

O'Callaghan's yawn dissipated the tension. 'How much longer are we going to be here? I've got a busy day in front of me.'

Birley seemed not to hear, still watching Raven. 'I wish I could make up my mind about you,' he said.

'I know exactly how you feel,' Raven answered.

Birley picked up his pen from the table. 'If you change your mind, you know where to reach me.'

'Change my mind about what?' asked Raven.

'Helping me. But you won't, will you?'

Raven just looked at him. He trusted none of them, not even this man. They closed ranks on each other's villainy in the name of loyalty.

'Get him out of here, will you,' Birley said to the lawyer. Frustration showed on his face. 'The station sergeant has his car keys. And keep him available. The Murder Squad will want a statement at some time or other.'

Raven pushed the swing door open. He dragged the damp air deep into his lungs. He could see the Commander talking to Cooney in the charge-room. Raven opened the car door for his friend. Headlamps shafted up Lucan Place.

'That's an experience not to be repeated,' Raven said feelingly.

O'Callaghan shivered and wound up the window. 'I've got to get back to bed. I'd just taken a sleeping pill when the police called.'

Traffic lights held them up at the bottom of Sydney Street. The clock outside Chelsea Town Hall read five past one.

The lawyer rocked in his seat-belt. 'What's going on between you and Kirstie? She's been ringing my office all day. Had I any idea where you were and all the rest of it. She said that you hadn't been home all night.'

'That's right,' Raven had smoked too much and his throat was dry. 'We had an argument. I don't have to tell you what the argument was about.'

The lights changed and he turned left into Old Church Street. The light was on in the courtyard. Maureen's car was parked there. O'Callaghan adjusted the scarf round his neck.

'I've got a feeling that we're being run away with, John. Maybe it's time to apply the brakes.'

'You're not driving,' said Raven. 'I am. Leave the brakes to me.'

He waited until his friend was safely inside the house. The courtyard light was extinguished. Friendship was the least complicated form of love. He parked in the cul-de-sac, looking across at the boats on the river. He no longer doubted that Cooney was the killer. The man had been clever enough to cover his tracks. The only real evidence against him had vanished with the porter. Raven had felt Cooney's contempt as the pair of them stood in the Interview Room. Cooney the untouchable. The only thing missing was the motive for the killings.

Raven locked up the Saab and walked to the end of the cul-de-sac. As he waited for a gap in the traffic, a Porsche Targa slid down the slope in front of the pub and stopped in front of Raven. A window was lowered.

'Get in the car!'

Raven leaned forward, balancing the pose with his shoulders. It was too dark to make out the driver's face. The passenger door was close to the pavement.

'There's a gun pointing at your stomach,' the voice said. 'Get in!'

Raven hesitated. Cars were passing in both directions. His only chance was to run for the cover
beyond the pub car park. Just one concentrated burst
of speed was all it needed.

'Don't be a fool!' warned the driver.

Raven could see the gun now and the man who
was holding it. The barrel was trained on Raven's
belly. He lowered himself into the passenger seat.
Raven's nostrils recognised the man's cologne immediately.

The driver's handsome face was hard. 'Paul Zeller.
Dragoti's my uncle.'

A door banged in the wind somewhere behind the
silent pub.

'My uncle died at six o'clock this evening,' the
driver said. 'That makes it family business.'

Raven cleared his throat but his voice was still
rough. 'You're talking to the wrong man. I've got no
idea what you mean.'

'You know,' said Zeller. 'You don't forget a million
and a quarter pounds worth of diamonds that easily.'

The car park perched a dozen feet above the
Embankment. There was a clear view of the boats
beyond. A light was burning in Raven's bedroom.

'You're talking to the wrong man,' Raven repeated.
'You were talking to the wrong man when you came
on the boat. I know nothing about any diamonds.'

'You're a liar,' said Zeller. 'I'm holding you people
responsible for my uncle's death.'

Raven spoke despairingly. 'Look, I can hear what
you're saying but it doesn't make sense! How can I
make you believe it? I don't know your uncle and I
know nothing about any diamonds.'

His heart faltered as the barrel of the gun lifted
slightly. A wave of self-pity washed over him. He

was about to die on a wet and windy car park without even knowing why.

Zeller's voice leaked cold menace. 'You people might think you've out-smarted me. But you're wrong. If I have to kill you, I will, depend upon it.'

'This is a nightmare,' said Raven, shaking his head.

Zeller's attitude changed very suddenly. 'We've got to be reasonable men, you and I. Forget Cooney. This is between you and me. You get twenty-five per cent of my uncle's property, no questions asked. If not, you go and your wife goes. You've got twenty-four hours to think it over.'

Raven moistened his lips furtively. Just open the door and walk away slowly.

The look in Zeller's eyes emphasised his sincerity. 'I'll kill you if I have to, Raven. The law won't help you. Deal with Cooney whichever way you want. Call me when your mind's made up. It's your last chance.'

A card with a telephone number on it dropped into Raven's lap. He put it in his pocket and pulled back the door catch. It looked a long way to the car park exit. He started to walk, thinking of something he had once heard. The impact of a bullet was felt before the ears accepted the sound of the shot. The banging of the door followed him down the slope to the pavement. He dashed across the road and down the steps. He looked back from the deck to the car park. The Porsche was no longer there. He turned the key in the lock and stepped into warm and familiar darkness. He was halfway to the kitchen when the bedroom door opened. Kirstie stood on the threshold, her feet bare, dressed in a pair of blue pyjamas. Her hair hung loose to her shoulders. She leaned against the wall, smiling at him. He held his arms wide and she came to him. He lifted her up, putting his lips on hers and swinging her round in a circle. Then he put her down very gently.

'Not a word!' he warned. 'Not one single word! We'll talk in the morning.'

Her eyes were anxious. 'A policeman was here asking for you.'

'In the morning,' he repeated. 'I'm going to take a bath.'

He soaked himself in the tub for half-an-hour, towelled himself dry and found a clean nightshirt in the airing cupboard. He took the shotgun from its case in the kitchen. The rain was blowing in squalls outside. Kirstie was lying in bed, her hair fanned over the pillows. She followed his movements as he checked the safety-catch and placed the shotgun on the floor. He slid into bed beside her. She reached up to extinguish her reading lamp, speaking in a very small voice.

'Am I allowed to ask just one question?'

'If I can answer with yes or no.'

The light went out. 'Do you still love me?'

'Yes,' he said. He could have elaborated but the rules were his own. Their lips clung together for a second, her touch on the back of his neck as soft as a rabbit's tail. They were asleep within minutes, fitted together like spoons, the shotgun on the floor beside them forgotten.

He woke to the inevitable sound of rain. The radio was playing in the kitchen. He smelled bacon frying. He turned on his back, stretching, refreshed after a dreamless sleep. His wife came through with a tray. He struggled upright.

'Bacon and eggs!' he said appreciatively. 'I'm being

spoiled.'

She watched while he ate. When he had finished, he wiped his mouth.

'I go first,' he announced and went into a straightforward account of the preceding twenty-four hours. She listened without interrupting, closing her eyes from time to time. The interlude with Zeller seemed to make the most impression on her. Suddenly she left the room. She came back holding some of the snapshots he kept in his desk.

'There's your answer,' she said. 'I left him alone while I talked to Hank.'

It was her turn to explain. He swung himself out of bed and took the tray into the kitchen. Kirstie followed him. He drank another glass of juice.

'I'll tell you what your visitor looked like,' he said. 'A little over six feet, blond hair and weird eyes. Wearing a dark-blue trenchcoat.'

It was a moment before Kirstie nodded. 'He showed me his warrant card. Detective Sergeant Cooney.'

'That's him,' said Raven. He pulled a pack of Gitanes from the carton in the kitchen dresser. 'He doesn't have a care in the world. You should have seen him last night. He's sitting on a million pounds worth of diamonds and he's killed three people but who's going to prove it! That's what he keeps telling himself!'

Her fingers found the jade heart she wore round her neck.

'It's horrible to think about. That man, killing all those people and sitting here on the boat.'

He tried to blow a smoke ring and failed again. 'Now we know the motive, the whole thing hangs together. Guerin brought the diamonds into the country. Slade and Cooney were the messenger boys. They kill Guerin and Cooney gets rid of Slade.'

She lit a cigarette of her own. 'Why hasn't Cooney taken off? That's the thing that puzzles me. Staying here doesn't make sense.'

The rain beyond the window showed no sign of slackening. 'Think of it as a poker game,' said Raven. 'Cooney's the man with the good cards. He won't leave the table while he's ahead. There's no reason. I can see that.'

'So what are you going to do?'

'Shave,' he said shortly. That done, he dressed in the cords he had worn on the previous day together with a clean flannel shirt.

Kirstie was in the sitting-room. She made the last stand he expected, wheedling as she straightened his collar.

'Let's get hold of Patrick, darling. This thing's out of hand now and it is his problem. *Please*, John.'

He bent down and tied his shoe-laces. 'If it hadn't been for you that woman would still be alive. Have you thought about that?'

She flushed as though he had struck her. 'That's a terrible thing to say.'

'But it's true,' he replied. 'Think about it. You're the one who invited Cooney on the boat. You played right into his hand. He must have sat there thinking what a pair of klutzes we were. Beryl Slade was dead the moment he went through my desk.'

She walked tight-faced into the bedroom. She emerged fifteen minutes later wearing a dark blue skirt and cream shirt. She sat on the sofa, next to him.

'Do you *really* think I'm responsible for that poor woman's death?'

The look in her eyes stabbed his heart. 'We're all

responsible,' he answered. 'Cooney wanted to frame me. I was just lucky. I could have been locked up for months answering questions.'

Her mascara was beginning to run. Her face was miserable.

'God knows why I married you.'

He shook his head at her. 'This notion's beginning to be an obsession with you. You married me because you loved me. It's normal enough. Together through thick and thin, remember?'

She wiped her eyes with a tissue, caught between laughter and tears.

'Do you know what that look on your face is called?'

He glanced sideways at his reflection. 'Natural dignity?'

'Intransigence,' she replied. 'And you win.'

He looked at his watch. It was almost nine o'clock. 'There are a lot of things I've got to do. Meet me at four o'clock. Peter Jones, inside the main entrance.'

The door slammed behind her. He called Jerry Soo's home number, catching him on his way out.

'One quick favour, Jerry. Can you find out if Cooney's on duty this weekend.'

'Should be no problem,' said Soo. 'How will I let you know?'

'Leave a message with Patrick. Just yes or no is enough.'

He found his mackinaw, an umbrella and a pair of overshoes and squelched up Oakley Street. It was no day to have to battle for existence. The faces he passed were glum and averted. People were waiting in the foyer of Chelsea Town Hall. The libraries were not yet open. No eating or drinking were allowed inside. Students hid their sandwiches and Thermos flasks under their text-books. There was the usual complement of those seeking shelter, the destitute with no other place to go. A saloon bar major was discussing the weather with his female counterpart. A poster on the wall said *Help for the Single Parent.* There were times when Raven regretted Kirstie's decision not to have children.

The doors to the reference library opened. It had the reputation of being the best of its kind in the city. It was like being in a well-ordered club with arm-chairs, reading desks and directional lamps. The silence was absolute. Raven draped his coat on the back of a chair and asked a librarian for scrap paper. He found *Gardner on Extradition* in the legal department. He took the tome to his desk and switched on the lamp. Something Kirstie had said at the height of their quarrel still disturbed him. 'You're completely closed-off!' she had screamed, tears running down her cheeks. 'Closed-off in this ridiculous dream world of yours. This bloody public avenger number!' What he wanted to yell in return was that it had been like that for some time. That it had always been like that. But this was something that only he had learned to accept.

He opened the book on the desk in front of him. A note in the preface described the subject matter. *'Causing a person accused of a crime to be handed over to the authorities of a foreign jurisdiction where the accused would stand trial.'*

Raven read on. Extradition treaties between sovereign states were explained as being expressions of political bias as well as expediency. Some countries were prepared to surrender foreign nationals but not their own citizens. Others refused to give up any fugitive charged with an offence of a political nature.

Extradition was also witheld as a mark of extreme disfavour.

He began making his list, excluding countries in the British Commonwealth. Cooney would know that these were covered by the Fugitive Offenders Act. Spain was the first name he wrote. The treaty between Spain and the UK had lapsed in 1978. A footnote made the point that it would probably be renewed when Spain joined the Common Market. There was no treaty with any of the Communist countries, but Cooney was unlikely to choose one of these to hole up in. Raven thumbed on through the pages. Brazil was the classic refuge but there were a number of others. The Philippines, a few places in the far East, a couple in Central America, half-a-dozen in Africa. Raven added Brazil, the Philippines and Costa Rica to his list and returned the book to the shelf.

He took a taxi to the Portman Hotel, walked through the lobby and out into Upper Berkeley Street. He was reasonably sure that he was not being tailed but was taking no chances. He turned into a Georgian house with a fanlight over the door. O'Callaghan shared the premises with a firm of architects. There were five rooms in his suite. The reception area was decked out with Finnish office furniture and Gauguin reproductions. The girl at the desk slipped her headphones off and glanced at the switchboard.

'Patrick's on the phone.'

Raven gave her the smile she deserved. The girl was an ally and occasional confidante. He left his coat and umbrella with her and turned the door handle. The lawyer raised a warning finger. Raven dropped into a chair. An untidy man himself, the disorder in this room never ceased to amaze him. The floor was strewn with box-files, legal briefs and theatre programmes. There were photographs of O'Callaghan's family on the walls. An ikon studded with amethysts sported a dead carnation. Hanging on the back of the door were a tailcoat and pleated dress-shirt. Chaos obtained on the desk. Letters with cheques attached spilled from the trays. There were most of the day's newspapers, a box of Austrian chocolates, Egyptian cigarettes and a pair of elbow-length doeskin gloves.

The lawyer cradled the phone and yawned. 'I've got a message for you from Jerry. Yes. That's all he said.'

Raven cleared a space on the floor for his feet. 'Things are hotting up, my friend. I had what might be called an adventure after I dropped you off last night.'

The lawyer listened to Raven's account of the meeting with Zeller. His face grew longer by the minute. He rubbed the ends of his fingernails on his patterned silk waistcoat.

'A million and a quarter pounds worth of diamonds! I find this hard to believe, John.'

'The others didn't,' said Raven.

The lawyer pulled a cigarette from the box and lit it nervously.

'No, no. I don't like this one little bit. It doesn't even make sense. Peter Guerin wasn't a crook.'

'How would you know,' Raven retorted. 'Because he paid your bills? Bullshit! The man was smuggling diamonds through customs.'

O'Callaghan stared at the end of his cigarette. 'I told you last night. Things are getting out of hand. It's time for the proper people to take over.'

'You mean the police?' Raven larded the suggestion with sarcasm. 'What are you going to say to them? You didn't like the way they were handling the case and asked your old friend Raven to make some enquiries? That ought to go down very well.'

'But I've got to do something,' the lawyer protested. 'I had no idea what you were getting into.'

'Hang on,' said Raven. '*You* produced me, remember. I'm not asking you to take your life in your hands, Patrick. But you're not just going to walk away from things.'

The electric typewriter in the adjoining room clattered like a burst of machine-gun fire.

'Listen,' said Raven. 'Do you believe what I've told you about Cooney? Do you believe it or not?'

O'Callaghan nodded emphatically. 'Of course I believe it. The trouble's going to be proving a single word of it.'

'Don't you think I don't know that!' Raven answered. 'Cooney's got Birley charmed. You saw them together last night. If we showed our hand now Cooney would simply deny everything. There isn't a single thing that he couldn't turn round.'

O'Callaghan scratched his cheek thoughtfully. 'If only we could get hold of the porter. That's direct evidence that Cooney had visited Guerin.'

'At least you're admitting that Guerin was a rogue.' Raven could not help grinning.

O'Callaghan glanced at the door apprehensively. 'Keep your voice down,' he urged.

Raven pulled his chair a little closer. 'My hunch is that Cooney's just about ready to take off. When he does, he's going to be carrying those diamonds. I'm going to see that he gets the incentive.'

O'Callaghan's cigarette burned unheeded in the ashtray. 'How can we be sure that these diamonds really exist?'

Raven looked at him disgustedly. 'For God's sake, three people are dead because of them. What do you want, a picture of Cooney wearing the bloody things?'

O'Callaghan was not too impressed. 'For a man who's been taking a lot of stick you sound very confident. What exactly is this plan of yours?'

'That's something you're better off not knowing,' said Raven. 'What I want from you is help. I need you to get hold of one of these people you know in the Home Office. Or that guy on *The Times*. He'd do. It doesn't matter who it is as long as the man carries some clout and is trustworthy.'

O'Callaghan ran a finger round the inside of his collar. 'I find this ironical. I start off with the best intentions in the world and finish up being involved in a mess like this!'

Raven respected his friend's sudden qualms and did his best to allay them.

'What you're doing now is helping me nail a cop who's killed three people. No more, no less. You have to come up smelling like attar of roses.'

The lawyer took a deep breath. 'Suppose I manage to get hold of someone. How much do I tell him?'

'Everything,' answered Raven. 'But no names until I give you the word. The first thing you have to do is get him interested.'

O'Callaghan raised his head. 'Can you imagine how this is going to sound?'

'Shit!' said Raven, his patience exhausted. 'What's the matter with you, for God's sake! I'm going to catch Cooney with the goods on him. But I need insurance. Someone who's prepared to listen and act. Are you with me or not?'

'I don't seem to have much choice, do I?' the lawyer said wryly.

'I was hoping that you'd be the one to say it.' Raven pulled the phone across the desk. 'Keep quiet while I make this call.'

He dialled the number that Zeller had given him. 'Raven', he said. 'I'll be at your place at ten o'clock tomorrow morning.' He put the phone down quickly and looked at his friend.

'I have to go,' O'Callaghan said, looking at his watch. 'I'm in court at eleven.' He stuffed some papers and a Walkman tape set in his briefcase. He used this in court when waiting, headphones on like a man refreshing his memory from notes previously made. In reality he was listening to Wagner.

Raven stood up. 'Where can I find you if I need you?'

'I'll be here until a quarter-to-seven.' He nodded at the evening clothes hanging on the back of the door. 'We're going to the opera.'

Raven paused at the door. 'Don't let me down.'

O'Callaghan offered his cat-like smile. 'Have I ever let you down?'

Bulstrode Buildings turned out to be a dingy building in Covent Garden. The opposite side of the street had been demolished in some grandiose scheme for redevelopment. Hoardings hid the remaining rubble. There was a car park at the back, a pub on the corner. According to the electoral roll for the ward, two people lived at Cooney's address. The other person was his sister. Raven had a salt beef sandwich in a café in Crawford Street and was in Sloane Square at a quarter-to-four. He furled the umbrella and walked through the entrance to Peter Jones. The china and glass counters were doing brisk business, girls gift-wrapping the customers' purchases. Raven loitered on the mezzanine floor. He had a clear view of the square and the street outside. It was five minutes to four when a taxi drew up in front of the store entrance. Kirstie hurried inside, looking anxiously at her watch. Raven waited a few moments until he was sure that she hadn't been followed. Then he ran downstairs, took his wife's arm from behind and impelled her forward. He steered her through rolls of carpets and bedding and out through a side door into the King's Road. They waited at the bus stop and jumped on the first bus that came. Raven tendered some coins, keeping his eyes on the traffic behind as the bus lumbered towards Knightsbridge. Kirstie sat next to him, wedged into the corner. Her stockings and shoes were spattered with mud. They left the bus at the Hyde Park Hotel. Tea was being served in a room overlooking the park. A waiter brought Earl Grey and muffins. Kirstie poured and passed a cup across the table. Her face showed the misery of a woman who knows that she does not look her best.

'I'll make it up to you,' he said quickly.

She moved the heavy tea-pot with her strong fine-boned fingers.

'I know that look,' she said. 'It means that something terrible is going to happen to me. Let's get it over.'

'Do you think you can fake an English accent?'

'An English accent?'

'Cockney. Do me if you like. Anything.'

'Are you being serious?' his wife demanded.

'Dead serious. This whole thing's going to depend upon your performance.'

She took a compact from her bag and studied her

face in the mirror. 'There's one thing I can truthfully say,' she observed, putting the mirror away. 'Life with you can never be said to be dull.'

'That's important,' he said and he meant it. 'We're going to light a squib under Cooney's tail, my love.'

The pulse beat in her neck made her somehow more vulnerable. 'Did you see Patrick?'

He nodded. 'We're getting the sort of help that you like.' The room was filling with women with loud assured voices. 'Let's get out of here,' he said.

He left some money on the table and draped Kirstie's mac round her shoulders. She wore it like a sable wrap. A taxi deposited them at the end of Shepherds Bush market. The street was lined with stalls lit by bottled gas and portable generators. Business was brisk in spite of the downpour. It was a mixture of people and the food that they ate. Cockneys were selling exotic fruits and vegetables. There were halal and kosher butchers, Greek and Italian bakers. West African matrons, as gaudy as macaws, slopped along with women in spangled saris. It was a cheerful and vulgar scene with music blaring out of every other doorway.

The Ravens stopped in front of a display of video machines and radios. The window was protected by a steel grille. Attached to the grille was a card giving notice that no Russian appliances would be repaired. A buzzer sounded as Raven pushed the door open. A huge man dressed in dirty overalls lumbered out of a back room. He inspected Raven and shook his head.

'Oh God!' he exclaimed. Then he lifted Raven in a gorilla hug, kissed his forehead and set him down again. He transferred his attention to Kirstie and lifted her hand with courtly gesture.

'You know one another,' Raven reminded. 'Jerzy

Keglevic.'

'I am certainly not forgetting,' said Keglevic. 'You are married with trouble, Madame. This man is dangerous.'

He reversed the legend in the window, presenting the *Closed* sign to the street. He ushered them into the workroom. A framed diploma hung above a bench covered with electronic components. It attested twenty years service with Decca Experimental Station. Next to it was a photograph of a younger Keglevic wearing RAF uniform. A statuette representing the Black Virgin of Cracow gazed out benignly.

The Pole's smile revealed a bank of gold fillings. 'You want coffee or vodka, perchance?'

Both Kirstie and Raven shook their heads.

'Then what I can do for you?' The Pole's slate-coloured eyes were curious.

'You gave me a car-bug some years ago. You told me to get rid of it when I'd finished. I need another one, Jerzy.'

'You see what I am telling you,' Keglevic said to Kirstie. 'Always this man is looking for trouble.'

He unlocked a cupboard, then turned, holding two small objects in his enormous hands. The transmitter was the size of a silver dollar with a powerful magnet built into one side. The oblong receiver was slightly larger with a dial calibrated in units of fifty metres. Keglevic touched a switch on the transmitter and a bleeping sound filled the workshop.

'Japanese,' he said. 'No interference on other circuits. Nobody see, nobody know. You are taking and giving back.'

Raven dropped the device in his mackinaw pocket. 'We've got to get out of here, Jerzy. How's Hanka?'

The Pole shrugged. 'Is old woman. Fifty-four. Is

always talking why we don't have children.'

He proffered his hand. Raven took it and smiled. 'We'll talk to you soon, Jerzy. And thanks.'

Keglevic kept Raven's hand in his own. 'You need help?'

'No,' said Raven. 'Saint Jude's taking care of things. But thanks all the same.'

The rain outside fell in stair-rods. The street was slippery with rotting fruit. They hurried towards Shepherd's Bush Green, crouched under the umbrella. A taxi responded to Raven's frantic waving.

'Cheyne Walk,' said Raven and closed the partition. His wife's eyes were quizzical as he showed her how the device in his pocket worked. The transmitter was attached to the underneath of a car and held in place by the magnet. The pointer on the dial registered the distance between the car and the vehicle that was following it.

Most of the boats were showing lights. Only the *Albatross* lay in total darkness. A note from Mrs Burrows was propped on the kitchen dresser.

A man phoned but he wouldn't leave no name nor message

Ada Burrows

Raven dialled the lawyer's office. 'Have you been calling the boat?'

'No,' said the lawyer. 'But I'm glad I got hold of you. I talked to Henry Villiers and he's definitely interested. But I'm going to have to give him some names.'

'Who is he?'

'Assistant director at the Department of Public Prosecutions.'

'Jesus Christ!' said Raven. 'The Establishment again.'

'Not this chap,' said O'Callaghan. 'The police busted his son on a dope charge. The kid was seventeen, smoking some grass at a concert. Henry's not a forgiving man.'

'Do what you think is right,' said Raven. 'But not a move until I give the word. And don't let this guy out of your sight. We may need him soon.'

'I've already told him. He's staying in London for the weekend. I hope I'm not making a fool of myself.'

'You keep your end up and I'll take care of mine.'

Kirstie came into the kitchen. She had changed into her jeans and suede jacket.

'Here's the plan,' he said. 'We're going to plant this bug under Cooney's car. If he's not there we'll wait until he is.'

He felt the apprehension running from her hands to his.

'But he's seen us both.'

He gripped her fingers even tighter. 'Don't worry about it. I know what I'm doing. Trust me. Sit down.'

She sat, facing him across the table. 'OK,' he said. 'Let's try the English accent.'

They talked for half-an-hour, Kirstie doing her best to sound like a Cockney, Raven correcting her faults.

'That'll do,' he said, glancing at the clock. 'Don't get drawn into conversations. Just stick to the script.'

They drove to Covent Garden and parked near the Underground Station. Raven switched off the lights and nodded at the gloomy façade of Bulstrode Buildings.

'I'll be back in a couple of minutes,' he said and left the car for the street.

Paper flapped on the hoardings, buffeted by wind

and rain. Raven ducked under the barrier and ran for the line of parked cars. He crouched by the side of the Jaguar, feeling beneath the chassis. The magnet lodged the tiny transmitter on the casing of the drive-shaft. The metal was still warm to the touch. He hurried back to Kirstie.

'Pray that it works,' he said fervently. He switched on the receiver. The needle swung across the dial and the receiver emitted a steady bleeping sound.

Raven switched off and put the set in Kirstie's bag.

'It's up to you, now,' he said quietly.

They waited in the Underground station until one of the phones was free. He pulled her close briefly and crowded into the booth with her. He dialled the number and handed the phone to Kirstie. He heard Cooney answer.

'I saw you last night in Beryl Slade's house,' said Kirstie.

Silence reigned for a few seconds. Then Cooney again. 'Who is this?'

'I'm Beryl's friend.'

'Where are you speaking from?'

'I'm not going to tell you that, am I?' Kirstie was doing a good job with the accent.

'I don't even know what you're talking about.' Raven recognised the anxiety in the other man's voice.

'Then why don't you put the phone down,' Kirstie challenged. Cooney stayed on the line. 'Beryl's dead,' said Kirstie. 'Nothing's going to bring her back. I want to get out of this stinking country. I need money. Not a lot. Five thousand pounds. I know you can get it.'

'You've got to be reasonable,' Cooney urged.

Kirstie tinkled a derisive laugh. 'I'll call you the

same time tomorrow and tell you how to get the money to me. It'll be the last you ever hear of me.'

She put the phone down and wriggled round to face Raven.

'How did I do?'

'You were brilliant,' he said and hurried her back to the car.

They sat with the lights out, watching the expanse of wet tarmac behind Bulstrode Buildings. Head-lamps flared suddenly. The Jaguar turned left into the one-way system.

'Get that thing going,' said Raven.

Kirstie opened her bag and the bleeping began. She leaned forward as the Saab moved in pursuit, peering through the space cleared by the windscreen-wipers.

'I can see him!' she said. 'Behind that bus!'

'Don't lose him,' said Raven. 'Keep your eye on him.'

There were three cars between the Jaguar and the Saab as the traffic flowed slowly south, down Charing Cross Road into Trafalgar Square. Raven maintained his distance. The lights changed as he made his approach, trapping him on the red. The Jaguar was already under Admiralty Arch and head-ing towards Buckingham Palace.

'Shit!' said Raven, shaking his head with frustra-tion. The bleeping continued from Kirstie's lap. The pointer on the dial traced the course of the Jaguar. It was three hundred yards away and travelling steadily. Green replaced red. Raven gunned the Saab forward. By the time they reached the end of the Mall the Jaguar was no more than a hundred yards in front.

'I've got him,' said Kirstie. Raven saw nothing but blurred lights in lashing rain.

He steered into the free-for-all at Hyde Park Corner.

'He's going left towards Belgrave Square,' Kirstie said excitedly. She was still leaning forward, her face almost touching the windscreen.

There were fifty yards between the two cars by now. They continued like this, down Sloane Street and into King's Road. The Jaguar's brake-lights came on suddenly, the indicator showing a right turn intended. The manoeuvre caught Raven by surprise. It was too late to do anything but continue. He averted his face as they passed the stationary Jaguar. Cooney was looking in the opposite direction. Red lights showed ahead at the junction of Beaufort Street. Nothing was coming their way. Raven wrenched the wheel over hard. The Saab rolled and regained equilibrium.

Kirstie's hand gripped Raven's knee. 'There's a cop right behind us,' she warned.

Raven looked up at the driving mirror and pulled in to the kerb. The white-helmeted traffic policeman rode past and propped his machine.

'Get that thing out of sight,' Raven said hurriedly.

Kirstie whipped the receiver into her bag. The copper walked back towards the car, his protective clothing glistening in the light from the headlamps. Raven wound down his window. The cop looked inside the car.

'Is this your vehicle, sir?'

'Yes, it is.' Raven produced his licence and insurance certificate.

The officer peeled off his gauntlets and laid them on the car roof. He studied the documents then looked up. His wave indicated the two lines of cars, all except the Saab facing in the same direction.

'Don't you know this is a one-way street?' he enquired.

Raven drew a nervous breath. 'I'm sorry, officer. The truth is I just didn't notice it.'

'That's a good way to get yourself and the lady killed,' the cop said severely. 'The sign's big enough, surely.'

'I'm afraid it's my fault, officer.' This was Kirstie at her best, apologetic and very female. 'I was supposed to be doing the piloting.'

The cop took another look at her. 'You drive, you do your own piloting, Madam.' He was young and plainly impressionable. 'Where are you people making for anyway?'

'We're on our way to the movies.' Kirstie's voice was full of contrition.

Rain bounced from the policeman's shoulders. Then the radio came to life on his BMW. He returned Raven's papers.

'Take this as a warning,' he said. 'And keep your eyes open in future.'

He walked off and straddled his machine. The engine growled and the policeman roared off into the King's Road traffic. Kirstie lit a cigarette. Her fingers were shaking in the flame of the lighter.

'I can't do this,' she said. 'I'm trying hard but I can't.'

He took the cigarette from her fingers and dropped it through the open window.

'Pull yourself together, darling. You're wonderful. We're going to split up. You stay in the car and cover the streets from here to Old Church Street. I'll go the other way. Don't stop if you see the Jaguar. Just remember where it is. I'll meet you in half-an-hour on the corner of Park Walk and Fulham Road.'

He took the receiver from her bag and switched on. The bleeping was constant. The needle located the Jaguar less than four hundred metres away.

He collected his hat and umbrella from the back seat. 'We've had worse and survived,' he said, leaning back through the window. 'It's all going to be all right, Kirstie.'

He watched the Saab until it had turned the corner, then walked towards Beaufort Street. Wet pavements reflected the lights from the street lamps. Few pedestrians braved the weather. He stopped under a lamp and checked the receiver. The needle showed that the distance had been cut to less than a hundred meters. He turned left into Elm Park Gardens. As he neared the Vale he stopped with a surge of triumph. The Jaguar was parked almost opposite him. Raven checked the numbers hurriedly. It was Cooney's car, no doubt of it. The Jaguar had been left in front of a house protected by burglar alarms and a closed-circuit television system. The camera was angled over the lighted doorway.

Raven put the receiver away and bent down by the front nearside wheel of the Jaguar. Moisture was running down his neck. He depressed the tiny piston in the valve with the tip of his ballpoint, releasing the air. The wheel subsided gently onto its rim.

He straightened up and looked around. There was no face at a window, no-one standing watching from a doorway. He started back towards Park Walk, half-running in his eagerness. He sheltered under the umbrella until the Saab appeared. He opened the door and threw the dripping umbrella on the back seat.

'We've got him,' he said exultantly. 'He's parked on the Vale and I've let one of his tyres down. All we have to do now is wait.'

She made no reply, staring straight in front of her.

'What's the matter?' he said. 'I tread on your foot or something?'

She turned her head slowly and he saw that her eyes were flooded with tears.

'It's you,' she said miserably. 'Whenever I see you like this I get scared.'

He kissed her cheek. 'Don't be! It's all over. All we do now is pick up the pieces.'

Cooney

Cooney stared into the mirror and inspected his teeth. Then he offered a smile to his reflection. Birley's voice bade him enter. The smell of Gold Block tobacco was tempered with the aroma of the mints the Commander was chewing. Cooney remained standing respectfully.

'Sit down!' Birley invited. 'I'm glad I got hold of you. I've been at the Yard all morning. A conference with the Assistant-Commissioner. I can't say I enjoyed the experience.'

'No, sir?' said Cooney. Monosyllables always worked well at times like this.

Birley locked his hands behind his neck. 'Let's deal with the watch first. Slade didn't buy it. It was sold by Van Cleef and Arpels in June of last year, a cash sale and the buyer never returned the guarantee form. So no address, unfortunately. However, the salesman's given a description of the purchaser. A man in his late twenties wearing a British Airways uniform. He paid cash in French francs!'

Cooney's face was charged with incredulity. He had been taking three Diludin capsules at a time instead of two and his thinking was sharp and inventive.

He steered the conversation away from the watch.

'What's happening about the post mortem, sir? Any news?'

Birley squeezed the corners of his mouth down. 'Nothing that helps, I'm afraid. From what Livingstone says Slade's neck was broken on impact. One thing that's bothering him is an area of heavy bruising at the top of the spinal column.'

Cooney draped one leg over another and frowned. 'Do we know when he got to the scene, sir?'

Birley extended a finger. 'Good thinking! That's what I asked. The body had been handled before Livingstone got there. Someone's going to have some explaining to do.'

Cooney nodded agreement.

The Commander made a note on a pad in front of him. 'He's going for accidental death. I imagine that'll be the Coroner's verdict. It's Murel and he doesn't waste time. It's next Tuesday, by the way, and they'll want you there.'

'I'll put it in my book,' said Cooney. He unbuttoned his blazer. The room was stuffy.

Birley popped another mint in his mouth and cracked it noisily.

'I can't get this business about Slade's wife out of my head. I'm not easily baffled but this thing defeats me. There was nothing worth stealing in the bloody place and she hadn't been sexually assaulted.'

'There's something I wanted to say about that, sir.'

Birley nodded abstractedly. 'The Murder Squad's got nothing to go on. They've had to be told about Slade, of course. The woman who found Mrs Slade is in the clear. She arrived, expecting to move in lock, stock and barrel. I'm sorry, I interrupted you.'

Cooney assumed the look of a man who knows that his judgement is biased.

'It's Raven, sir. I still think he's in there some-where. I'm sorry.'

Birley leaned back in his chair, looking at Cooney. 'I never told you this before, sergeant. The day after Slade was killed someone put your name and Slade's through the C.R. Eleven computer. The man who did it is an inspector who was with Raven at police college. They make no secret of the fact that they still see one another. This man asked for a character profile and service records.'

Cooney's amber eyes widened but he managed a smile. 'I suppose I ought to be flattered.'

'Don't you get the point?' the Commander said shrewdly. 'Raven's a menace. I don't believe for a minute that he's anyway involved in Slade's death. He's up to his usual tricks. If he's at the inquest we can assume the worst, Cooney. It's going to be the end of the division as far as we know it.'

'I can handle reporters,' said Cooney.

A look of pain spread over the Commander's face and he closed his eyes briefly.

'Please God it doesn't come to that. It isn't just my head on the block, it's everyone's! Are you on duty this weekend?'

Cooney struck what he hoped was the right note. 'I'm not, sir, no. But I can be if you need me.'

Birley shook his head quickly. 'A rest is what we all want. Not that I'm likely to get one but there's no reason why you shouldn't.'

'Thank you, sir.' It was difficult now to stop smiling. 'I thought of taking my sister to Kew Gardens.'

Birley was putting the things from the desk in a drawer. 'Wrong time of the year. What age woman is she?'

'Thirty-four and unmarried, sir.'

The Commander's smile was knowledgeable. 'Try a dance-hall, sergeant. It's a great place to get rid of unmarried sisters. I'll see you on Monday morning.'

The one man in the Squad Room vanished as Cooney came in. His relations with the others had been strained since Slade's supposed posting on special assignment. The truth of course would come out at the inquest. Cooney checked his locker and walked out into scudding rain. When he reached Bulstrode Buildings his sister's car was already parked there. He pulled alongside it and climbed the stairs. Teresa was in the sitting-room. She called but he went straight to his bedroom and closed the door. He stretched out on the bed for a moment, reviewing the interview with Birley. The news about Raven disturbed him. When he finally went through to the sitting-room, his sister was knitting, her legs festooned with wool. She charged straight into attack.

'If you're expecting to be fed tonight, you can go out for it. I'm sick and tired of making meals for someone who doesn't even have the manners to say that he won't be here.'

He changed channels on the television set. A short burst of music announced the six o'clock news. Only then did he speak to her.

'You've been poking around in my room again.'

'Poking around!' she repeated. 'It happens to be laundry day and clean clothes don't find their way into drawers by themselves.'

He poured himself a beer thinking how much he had always disliked her. His childhood had been jaundiced by her sanctimonious criticism. And now she looked forty, one of the sad sorority of amateur nuns inflicting their sour advice on the less righteous.

The newscaster's voice droned on. An oil-rig had sunk off Norway. The Israelis and Syrians were invading one another. He switched the set off.

His sister bit off a thread of wool, speaking with her mouth full.

'I got rid of all those empty bottles.'

He touched the end of his tongue to his lips but said nothing. His refusal to rise to the bait seemed to inflame her.

'You needn't think I don't know what's going on,' she said. 'You ought to be ashamed of yourself.'

'Know what you are?' he said. 'You're a nosy old bag.'

Anger suffused her face. 'From someone I've sacrificed my life for! Thank God the parents never lived to see it!'

He dropped the beer can in the kitchen waste basket and came back for more. She gave it to him gladly.

'You can take in others with the glib tongue and phoney smile, but I know you too well, Terry. You've got no feeling for anyone except yourself. And no respect either.'

He leaned in the doorway. 'How could I have respect for a woman like you?'

Her lips went white at the edges. 'If you'd worked a little harder at school you might have been able to find yourself a decent job.'

'I've got a decent job,' he said, grinning.

She bridled, the skeins of wool forgotten and tangled. 'Oh, I'm sure you enjoy it! Sneaking round corners and catching people out. It lets you mix with the riffraff you really like.'

The mynah bird made a belching noise. It was Cooney's only contribution to its instruction. He considered his sister calmly, trying to remember if he had ever loved her. He decided not. He had never loved anyone.

'One of these days I'm going to move out of here and really disgrace you, take up with some spade hooker.'

'No such luck,' she said bitterly. 'You know when you're well off.'

He was back in his bedroom when the phone there rang. The voice was a woman's.

'I say you last night in Beryl Slade's house.'

He sank down on the bed, unwilling to believe what he was hearing.

'Who is this?' he said.

'I'm Beryl's friend.'

His lips went dry. He forced himself back in time, reviving the dark street under rain, the desolate stretch of common beyond. No-one had seen him leave the house, he was sure of it. And yet . . .

The voice continued to talk, its import deadlier by the second. He put the phone down as if it were a phial of nitro-glycerine. Then he went into the bathroom and swallowed three Diludin capsules. His sister's voice sang out from the sitting-room.

'Who was that?'

He waited for the first rush from the drug.

'The station,' he answered. 'They want me there.'

She came from the sitting-room. She looked at him closely. 'Is there something wrong, Terry? You've gone a very peculiar colour.'

He managed to pull himself together. 'I'm all right. It's this business with Beryl Slade.'

She made a sound of disapproval high in her nose. She had met Slade's wife on one occasion and had taken an immediate dislike to her.

'I don't know why they waste their time,' she said.
'I'll probably be late,' he said and pulled on his
Burberry. He ran downstairs, switched on his headlamps and lifted the barrier. Once in Chelsea he
parked in the Vale. He walked to Beaufort Street with
his coat-collar up round his ears. He glanced up and
down the street before letting himself into the
hallway. Someone upstairs was playing an old Stones
record. He tiptoed up the stairs and unlocked his
room. Steam was leaking from the bathroom next
door. The street lamp outside threw a pattern of light
across the ceiling. He opened the cupboard and
carried the things inside to the bed, reassured by the
knowledge of what they stood for. The box of
diamonds, his passport and the flight ticket. He
dribbled some stones into his hand. Fire flashed in
his palm. He suddenly wanted to see the jewels in all
their glory. For that he needed light. He walked to
the window to draw the blind down. A man was
walking down the street in the direction of Radnor
Studios. The top half of his tall frame was concealed
beneath an umbrella but Cooney recognised the
loping walk at twenty yards. He moved away quickly
from the window and flattened his back against the
wall. His mouth was dry and bitter.

A bus lumbered by, the passengers on the top deck
on a level with Cooney's room. When he looked
down at the street again Raven had vanished.
Cooney slumped down on the bed, his morale
severely shaken. He was losing control of events.
Raven's appearance outside clinched matters. The
fact that he lived in the neighbourhood might explain
his presence, but the risk was too big for Cooney to
take. He had to get out of the country tonight, to pull
up stakes and run. There was nothing to stop him. By

Sunday morning he could be six thousand miles away.

Instinct and judgement told him to leave the Jaguar where it was. He remembered that Raven had friends at the Yard. He might well know the numbers on the car that Cooney was driving. The thought ran like a lighted fuse. Even the thought of leaving the house by the front door seemed insanity. There was no way of being sure that Raven was not sitting in one of the cars parked outside, waiting for Cooney to emerge. He stuffed the diamonds and documents into his pockets and opened the door a crack. The bathroom was empty. He went down the stairs very quietly, through the hall and down to the basement. A door there opened into the garden. The key was in the lock. Cooney unfastened the bolts. The door opened stiffly, dislodging a mat of wet leaves. He was beginning to show signs of strain. He sheltered as best he could, taking his bearings. The wall on his right led to the neighbouring garden. Beyond that was the street that ran at right angles to Radnor Studios.

He jumped for the top of the wall and clawed himself up, using hands and knees. He dropped in a muddy flowerbed. A dog barked inside the house. Then a light illuminated the shrubbery. A woman's head appeared at a window and vanished again. Cooney escaped by the side-entrance, his heart pumping at a furious rate. Flight was his sole thought now. A taxi deposited him at Victoria Station where he washed in the Gents, restoring respectability to his appearance. He waited his turn at a telephone in the concourse.

A woman's voice answered his call immediately. 'KLM. Good evening!'

'My name's Terence Cooney.' He spelled it out for

her. 'I've got a first class open ticket from Amsterdam to San Jose, Costa Rica. Can you get me on tomorrow's flight?'

'One moment, please. I'm putting you through to Passenger Reservations.'

The line clicked and Cooney repeated himself. He waited while the details were fed into the computer then the woman was back.

'That'll be fine, Mr Cooney. What passport do you hold?'

'British.' No visas were necessary.

'Fine,' she repeated. 'They'll validate your ticket at Schiphol Airport. Check-in time is one hour before take-off.'

He returned his ticket to his pocket with a feeling of having lost something. It took him only seconds to realise that he had mislaid the yellow folder that had enclosed his ticket. He couldn't remember seeing it since he'd bought it. Maybe he had left it behind at the studios. It had been dark in the room and his mind had been on other things. It was probably on the bed. He relaxed, reasoning that no-one would visit the room for three weeks.

A board outside the Sealink booking hall announced the suspension of jetfoils and hovercraft due to bad weather. A disconsolate line of travellers was waiting for the Dover–Calais boat train. Cooney turned on his heel, daunted by the prospect of a tedious trip on a bucketing ferry-boat. He had twenty-four hours before the plane left Amsterdam, but the sooner he was out of England, the better. He walked through the station and into the British Airways booking office. A clerk leafed through a compendium of airline schedules.

'Amsterdam, sir? There's only one flight left today.

Twenty-three hours forty from Heathrow. Do you want me to try for you?'

Cooney nodded.

The clerk punched some keys and scanned the result on his screen.

'No problem,' he said looking up. 'Pay the cashier if you please.'

The clerk was still offering assistance when Cooney collected his ticket.

'There's a bus leaves from outside every half-hour. Have a good flight.'

Cooney had no intention of putting himself on show for too long at the airport. He bought a toothbrush, razor and a roll of adhesive tape and walked into the Scotia Hotel. It was large and impersonal, a perfect place to kill the next hour or so. He had a word with the hall-porter, ordering a car to take him to the airport. He took a beer and sandwich to the corner of the bar and made himself inconspicuous in a corner. More Diludin capsules had restored his confidence. Whatever Raven or Zeller had planned for him they were too late. In another couple of hours he'd be out of the country. He leafed through some magazines, checking his watch from time to time. At twenty-five minutes past nine he strolled through to the lobby.

A dark-skinned man was standing there chatting to the hall porter who lifted a finger at Cooney.

'Your car, sir!'

Cooney followed the driver outside. The car was a white Ford Capri with mock tigerskin upholstery. A metal tag on the dashboard identified the driver: *Ram Dhaniram*. Cooney took a cigarette from his pocket. Checking-in could be a danger point. He leaned forward as the car turned west into the Cromwell

Road.

'Are you married, Mr Dhaniram?'

The Hindu glanced up at the rearview mirror, his expression slightly startled.

'No. Why?'

'Take my advice and don't,' said Cooney. 'You can do me a favour when we get to the airport. My ex-wife will probably be there. I don't want to see her. If you'd check-in for me and get my boarding-card it would be a help. I'll make it worth your while, of course.'

The Hindu had an incongruous Cockney accent. 'Where's she going to be?'

'That's the problem,' said Cooney. 'I've no idea. Her sister warned me that she'd be there. She pulls this sort of stunt once a month. Can't let me alone. Last time she came to the office and started abusing me.'

Vapour had formed inside the windows. The lights of the cars they were passing were lost in a watery haze. The driver appeared to be looking for flaws in Cooney's suggestion.

'Can't you get her nicked?' he asked suddenly.

'The police don't want it,' said Cooney. 'It's a domestic matter.'

'OK,' said the Hindu. 'I'll help you out but I don't want no problems.'

'You won't have problems,' Cooney assured him. He passed his ticket over the driver's shoulder together with the fare and a ten pound note. 'All you do is check-in for me. I'll take care of everything else.'

Both men fell silent. Tyres swished on the wet road. The windscreen-wipers flicked monotonously. It was a quarter to eleven when the hire-car approached the Terminal Buildings. A line of buses and cars waited outside.

'Let me out here,' Cooney said quickly. The driver pulled to the kerb. 'I'll see you at the bottom of the escalator,' said Cooney.

Electronically-controlled doors led to the check-in counters. The Hindu took his place in the queue. Cooney watched from a point of vantage, alert for any sign of danger. Plain clothes-men were dotted around the hall. The main business of the airport was conducted two floors above. Immigration and Customs, the banks and shops. The Hindu collected his boarding-card and left the counter. None of the plain clothes-men paid any attention as he moved towards the escalator.

Cooney came out from behind the pillar. Dhaniram pushed the boarding-card into his hand and was gone in a flash.

Cooney rode the escalator to the second floor. The first hurdle had been cleared. There were two more to come. He made his way through the crowd upstairs and entered the nearest lavatory. He locked himself in a stall and hung his jacket and Burberry on the back of the door. He took the diamonds from the box and wrapped them in lavatory-paper, making a flat package that he taped between his legs inside his boxer shorts. He pulled his trousers up, donned his blazer and Burberry and dropped the cardboard box in the refuse bin. The first few steps that he took were uncomfortable but by the time he reached the khaki-clad security guards he was walking normally. He produced his boarding-card and moved on to Immigration control. The Special Branch officer's eyes roved from Cooney to his passport. Cooney's description was listed as police officer. The man smiled and returned the passport.

'Business or pleasure?'

'A little bit of both, I hope,' Cooney answered.

His pulse-rate beat marginally faster as he neared the security check ahead. He stepped through the electronic metal-detector. A guard patted Cooney's pockets and body and waved him on. Cooney joined the others in the Departure Hall. Destinations and flight-times were shown on overhead screens.

Amsterdam was already posted. Gate Eleven. He locked himself in the lavatory again and retrieved the diamonds. He combed his hair in the mirror, smiling. He was home, Sweet Jesus! Home and dried! In half-an-hour's time he'd be airborne.

Raven

Raven and Kirstie had been sheltering in the doorway for half-an-hour. They were twenty yards away from the crippled Jaguar, waiting for Cooney to surface. Kirstie looked at her soaked shoes and shivered. Raven wrapped his arm round her shoulders and held her tight.

'Let's get out of here!'

They unfurled the umbrella and ran for the Saab. Kirstie pulled the sun-visor down and inspected her face in the mirror.

'God what a mess!'

She was trying to put her hair in some order. She pushed the sun-visor up with a gesture of defeat.

'I'm wet,' she said. 'And I'm scared. What I feel like doing right now is bursting into tears.'

He lowered his hand on her thigh, kneading the soft flesh gently.

'You're not going to burst into tears, my darling. You're going to help me nail Cooney. Kirstie, look at me!'

She turned her head and managed a tremulous smile. 'But of course, I'm so brave. You monster!'

'It's something I've got to do,' he affirmed.

'I know,' she said quietly and kissed his cheek. 'I'm sorry for being such a bitch.'

They drove back to Covent Garden. 'This is it,' he said, looking across at the dreary wet buildings. 'If I can't make his sister see reason we're sunk.'

He walked across the poorly-lit entrance. A board on the wall gave the location of tenants. The Cooneys were up on the second floor. Raven climbed stone stairs that smelled of carbolic. A naked light hung on the landing. There was only one door. Raven pressed the bell. Footsteps rustled inside.

'Who is it?' asked a woman's voice.

'John Raven, Miss Cooney. I have to talk to you about your brother. It's very important.'

She opened the door a fraction. The woman bore little resemblance to her brother. She was dark, dowdy and suspicious.

'What about my brother? Who are you, anyway?'

She was wearing a shapeless wool dress and fur-fabric slippers. He was suddenly conscious of his own appearance, the soaked muddied sneakers and wrinkled trousers.

'Look,' he said. 'We don't have much time. My wife's downstairs in the car. We can talk there if you'd prefer it.'

'Not until I know who you are,' she said firmly.

'I've already told you my name,' he pleaded. It was useless to attempt any further explanation. 'This is really a matter of life and death.'

It took her a moment to make up her mind. She opened the door, letting him into a hallway warmed by a paraffin heater. A television set was on in the sitting-room. She switched it off and sat across the velour-covered table from him, her hand close to the telephone.

He kept his eyes on her face, sparing her nothing. 'Your brother has killed three people, Miss Cooney

165

including the man he used to work with.'

Her hand flew to her throat and her face lost colour.

'I'm sorry to tell you like this,' he said. 'I had no option. I think that he's on his way out of the country. I need your help to stop him.'

Her hand crept towards the telephone. 'Who are you? Where do you come from?'

'It doesn't matter, Miss Cooney. You've got to trust me.'

A mynah bird screeched in the corner. She rose and threw a blanket over its cage.

'Why aren't the police here themselves?'

Something in her manner encouraged him. 'Because he's managed to fool the lot of us. The people he works with, you, me – everyone! Listen to me, Miss Cooney. Your brother's killed three people and do you know what for? I'll tell you. A million and a quarter pounds' worth of diamonds! Do you want him to escape? Is that what you want?'

She stared at him, dull-eyed, digesting the enormity of what he was saying. Then she shook her head, somehow managing to achieve dignity.

'You don't have to tell me about my own brother. I brought him up. I know Terry's faults. He has no scruples, but I can't believe that he'd take human life.'

Looking at her, he felt compassion but he chose the words for their shock value.

'Your brother shot one man in the back of the head. And he bludgeoned Slade's wife to death. Those two we can be sure about, Miss Cooney. We can't let him get away with it and time's running out on us. Please will you help me?'

She shut her eyes tight, pushing the image away.

Tears squeezed through her misery and rolled down her cheeks. She seemed to draw unexpected strength from somewhere.

'He's still my brother, whatever he's done.'

Raven took a deep breath, filled with frustration and anger. His gesture took in the cross that she wore on her breast, the painting of Saint Francis of Assisi.

'What sort of Christian *are* you?' He was close to shouting. 'Are you telling me that you condone murder because it's your brother?'

She broke suddenly, covering her face with her hands.

'You don't have to do a thing,' he said gently. 'Just show me his room.'

She took her hands away, a sad dowdy woman with the longing to be told that she was mistaken. Then she rose very slowly and led Raven through the kitchen.

'That door there,' she said, pointing.

He took her hand spontaneously. 'I can't stop you from calling the police but I can tell you this much if you do. By the time the truth is established your brother will be out of the country. It's up to you.'

He turned away, knowing that there was no more that he could do. He opened the door and found the light-switch. The room looked like a schoolboy's. A single bed was pushed against the wall with a telephone on a chair next to it. A Beatles poster from their Hamburg days hung on the wall. The books were all paperbacks. Chandler and Le Carre. Raven worked hurriedly, searching the clothes in the wardrobe. He found nothing of interest there nor in the chest of drawers. There was an empty bottle of Diludin tablets under the bed. He straightened his back dispiritedly as the door opened. Teresa Cooney stood there, her face a mask of stone.

Her hand came from behind her, holding out a yellow KLM ticket envelope.

'Is this what you're looking for?'

He opened the envelope. Tucked inside was a list of addresses. They were all in San Jose, Costa Rica. He grabbed the phone from the chair and dialled.

'KLM. Good evening, may I help you?'

'Can you give me the time of your next flight from Amsterdam to San Jose, please?'

He waited for the answer, hearing the pulse in his head beating. The voice was precise, like that of the Speaking Clock.

'The next flight is tomorrow evening, sir, leaving Schiphol Airport at seventeen hours twenty.'

'One more thing,' he said quickly. 'Do you know if there's a plane from here to Amsterdam tonight?'

She gave him the reply he expected. 'Twenty-three hours forty, sir. British Airways Flight Two four six.'

He dropped the phone and shoved the yellow envelope into his pocket. Tears ravaged the woman's face. Her voice was barely audible.

'What will they do to him?'

'They'll give him a trial,' said Raven. 'It's more than he gave the others.'

He brushed past her, unwilling to waste more time. He had to get hold of O'Callaghan and arrange for help at the airport. He flew down the stairs to the street. Kirstie's face was a glimmer behind the rainspotted windscreen. Raven opened the driver's door, too late to notice the Porsche at the end of the street.

Paul Zeller uncoiled in the back of the car. The gun in his hand was pointing directly at Kirstie's head. It was the same gun he had carried before. His voice was flat and emotionless.

'Just do what I say. The first wrong move and I blow her head off.'

Kirstie's eyes met Raven's helplessly. The gun was only inches from her head.

'You're making the biggest mistake of your life,' said Raven. The words sounded over-dramatic and hackneyed.

'Just drive,' said Zeller. 'Campden Hill.'

Raven put the Saab in motion. 'You're making a big mistake,' he repeated.

'We all are,' said Zeller. 'Now shut up and drive.'

Raven could smell the drink on his breath. He turned right into Phillimore Gardens and began the long ascent. The gun behind moved slightly, indicating a small block of flats on the left.

'Pull up in the entrance!' Zeller dropped a key in Raven's lap. 'Number three, the first on your left. Walk straight in there.'

Wall-lamps bathed the lobby with soft light. It was quiet and warm. Mirrors reflected Raven's image as he crossed and unlocked Zeller's door. There was no chance to use the phone on the hall table. Zeller and Kirstie were already in the lobby, walking close together like lovers. Zeller closed the door and a shove sent Kirstie staggering. She collapsed on the sofa.

'You sit beside her!' Zeller ordered, pointing at Raven. Zeller was wearing tweed trousers with a fawn cashmere sweater. The rest of his apparel must have been left in the Porsche. He drew the curtains and poured himself a Scotch. A record had stuck on the stereo and turned uselessly, the stylus clicking in the speakers. Zeller examined Raven sombrely.

'I don't know what makes a man like you tick. Or

whether you even have any loyalties.'

Kirstie spoke up, the skin on her face dead white against the freckles that banded her nose.

'You're not being fair . . .' she began but her voice lost confidence.

Zeller finished his drink. His smile was no more than a rictus.

Raven moved closer to his wife. There was nothing he could do to protect her but he wanted her near.

'I told you before, we have nothing to do with your diamonds.'

Zeller refilled his glass. 'I've lost the only real friend I ever had. Have you any idea what that means?'

Sweat was dripping down Raven's ribcage, cold to the skin.

'Look, my wife has nothing to do with any of this. If you'd give me a chance to explain . . .'

'You had your chance,' said Zeller. 'Your wife's part of your family as far as I'm concerned and that's what this is about. Family.'

There was a surreal quality about what was going on. As if it were happening to three other people.

'We're on the same side,' Raven said desperately. 'It should be us against Cooney not the other way round.'

Zeller put his glass down empty. The drink seemed to be having no effect upon him.

'My uncle died without even knowing that I was there with him. He just lay there like an animal with dribble coming out of his mouth. Have you any idea at all what that did to me?'

Raven had met desperate men in his life. Men without bluster whose very stillness carried the certainty of death. And this man was one of their company. He summoned what was left of his courage.

'There's nothing I can do if you've made up your mind to kill me. But there's something you ought to know. Cooney killed Guerin and Cooney killed Slade and his wife.'

The record continued to click in the speakers. Zeller's smile was derisory.

'What liars you people are! Not an ounce of loyalty to one another. You're about as low as you can get.'

Raven withdrew his hand from his pocket, displaying the yellow envelope.

'I can prove it.'

'Drop it!' said Zeller and turned to Kirstie. 'You pick it up!'

She bent forward and retrieved the KLM envelope and held it with trembling fingers.

'There's a list of addresses inside,' said Raven.

'Read it,' said Zeller.

She took out the piece of paper. 'Garfinkel Hermanos, Jewelers, Calle Columbus Eighteen, San Jose. Banco Central, Plaza Mayor, San Jose. Roberto Duarte, Ministerio Extranjero.'

Zeller studied their faces closely. 'Empty your pockets,' he said suddenly. 'Drop everything on the floor in front of you!'

Kirstie let the contents of her bag fall on the carpet. Lipstick and eye makeup, money and keys and the tiny bleeper. Raven added his own contribution. Zeller drew the bleeper closer with the toe of his shoe.

'What's this?'

'Half of a bugging device,' Raven answered. 'The other half's sitting under Cooney's car. We followed him from his home to Chelsea. That's where we lost him. I'm pretty certain that he had the diamonds stashed somewhere near there. There's a flight from Amsterdam to San Jose tomorrow evening and a flight from Heathrow to Amsterdam at eleven-forty tonight. Cooney's going to be on it.'

For the first time Zeller appeared to be aware of the record. He switched off the stereo.

'How do you fit in with all this? What's your connection with Guerin?'

Kirstie's nervous laugh was almost a giggle. 'I just hope you can make sense of the answer.'

Raven did his best with what he had. 'Guerin was a client of a friend of mine, a lawyer called Patrick O'Callaghan. Things seem to have developed from there.'

His wife moved her head sadly. 'The awful thing is that he's telling the truth.'

Zeller had the card Birley had given Raven in his hand. 'What about this?' Zeller demanded.

Raven shook his head. 'I said nothing. Birley's a cop and they tend to take care of their own, no matter what rank they hold. I speak from experience. I've gone somewhere else for help.'

'Where?' Zeller fired the word like a missile.

For the first time Raven saw a glimmer of assurance. 'Someone in the Director of Public Prosecutions Office. Someone who doesn't particularly like the police. He's a friend of O'Callaghan's.'

Zeller looked at the clock on the mantel. 'Where can you get in touch with O'Callaghan?'

'He's at the Royal Opera House.'

Zeller indicated the phone. 'Call him!'

There were three listings given in the telephone directory. Box office, stage door and management. Raven dialled the stage door number. A man's voice responded. Raven articulated clearly.

'This is an emergency. I'm trying to get hold of a Mr O'Callaghan.'

The voice repeated the name uncertainly. 'They're all on stage at the moment. It's the last act, see.'

The man was patently deaf. Raven bawled. 'He's in the audience! This is an . . .' the phone went dead.

'He hung up on me,' Raven said to Zeller.

The younger man stuck the pistol in his waistband, took the phone, dialled and spoke in a tone of courteous urgency. The menace had disappeared.

'My name is John Raven. You have a Patrick O'Callaghan in the audience. It's a matter of extreme urgency that he gets in touch with me. Tell him that I've gone to Heathrow to see Cooney. C o o n e y. That's right. Will you see that he gets this message before he leaves the theatre? It's a matter of life or death. Thank you!'

He cradled the phone. His voice was quiet and reasoned. 'They're going to page him just as soon as the curtain is down.'

Raven wiped his face. The sweat had extended to his neck and forehead.

'Now what?' he asked.

'Pick your things up,' said Zeller. 'I'm still not sure if you're lying or not but there's one way to find out.'

He grabbed a coat from the hall and led the way to the Saab. He opened the rear door for Kirstie and took the seat next to Raven.

'If this *is* another production, so be it. There's nothing else left to lose.'

There was something about the man that Raven found himself respecting, a kind of belated chivalry, almost companionship. Raven needed to say something but was uncertain how to phrase it.

'Every word I've told you is the truth,' was the best he could manage.

Zeller nodded indifferently. 'It'll make a change.'

They drove south and then west towards Chiswick, travelling along the elevated stretch of motorway. The giant office buildings and factory complexes were as brilliantly lit as concentration camps. Zeller just sat there, drumming his fingers on the dashboard. It was ten minutes to eleven. The slush thrown up by overtaking vehicles, the rain and murk, all seemed designed to delay them.

'I'm sorry about your uncle,' Raven said impulsively.

Zeller turned in his seat. 'Garbage! You're not sorry at all. He's just another crook to you. Do you think those diamonds were stolen?'

A warning flashed ahead, instructing drivers to slacken their speed. Raven lifted his foot off the accelerator, his eyes on the ribbon of road.

'I don't know what the hell to think,' he admitted.

Zeller seemed anxious to explain. 'Did you ever hear of Illicit Diamond Buying?'

It was a boyhood memory. 'I've read about it,' Raven answered.

'A crime invented by the Syndicate. It still goes on. The stones finish up in Europe and have to be sold under cover. It's legal enough out of South Africa but if the Syndicate gets to know about it, you're finished in the trade. Wiped out. My uncle took chances.'

It was as if Zeller were trying to justify his uncle's memory. When Raven made no comment he continued.

'Do you cheat on your income tax?'

Raven removed his eyes from the road momentarily. 'What kind of a question's that?'

'OK, you've got an accountant who does it for you.'

Raven swung onto the slip road that led to the airport. 'I don't know what the hell you're getting at.'

A match flared as Kirstie lit three cigarettes. She passed one to Zeller and one to her husband.

Zeller continued. 'My uncle brought diamonds into this country without paying tax on them, VAT, that is. This was meant to be his last venture. He was a good man who never did any real harm to anyone, no more a criminal than you are, Raven. He made one mistake. He trusted the wrong people.'

They were suddenly quiet, all three lost in their thoughts. The only sound was the drone of the engine.

'You're going to have a lot of questions to ask,' Raven said suddenly.

'True,' answered Zeller. His face in the half-light was almost amused. 'I imagine we both are.'

'My husband is used to it,' Kirstie said from the back. Her nervousness had completely gone.

Signs spiked the shoulder of the road. *Long Term Parking, Departures* and *Short Term Parking*. The traffic divided into two lanes. Left was the complex of airport facilities, to the right the multi-storey car park.

'Pull over here,' said Zeller. People were being unloaded in front of them. Raven obeyed and switched off the engine. Zeller's eyes showed the strain he was under.

'We must make a plan,' he said. It was almost an appeal not an order.

The clock on the dashboard showed five minutes past eleven. They had half-an-hour.

'I want Cooney,' said Raven.

'So do I,' admitted Zeller.

Raven understood. 'The first whiff of something wrong and he'll be off and running.'

'There are probably two thousand people in that building,' said Kirstie, leaning forward. 'Locating him isn't going to be that easy.'

Zeller nodded. 'And when we *do* locate him?'

'I think that's my problem,' said Raven.

Zeller pitched his cigarette butt through the window. 'I don't mean to be offensive, but you're in no shape to take on someone like Cooney.'

'Bravo,' Kirstie said softly.

'Don't think I don't understand,' said Zeller. 'I'm like you. I want to be there at the end. I want to see them put the cuffs on the bastard. It isn't the diamonds any more. I'd like you to know that.'

The Canadian voice from behind piped up again. 'Why are we wasting time? Patrick will have had the message. I say we go to the police.'

Raven removed the ignition keys. 'That's what we do.'

In spite of the hour the concourse was full of passengers, all of them apparently without direction. Tired tourists badgered equally tired counter-staff. Children slept or ran where they could. A couple of banks were still exchanging money. The shops and cafés were open. Raven drew the other two to one side. He no longer had qualms about Zeller. The die had been cast, the three of them bound in complicity.

'Wait here,' he said. A security guard gave him the information he asked for. He waved and the other two joined him. They ran up the staircase. It was thirteen minutes past eleven by now. They were still running when they reached the second floor. Each passing second seemed to destroy their purpose. They burst through a couple of swing doors into a glass-lined corridor. Below a waste of wet tarmac stretched on the left to winking lights at the ends of the runways. Other corridors led to embarcation chutes where planes waited to be loaded. A door bore the single word *Police*. Raven pushed it open.

A thin-featured young man was sitting at a desk behind a counter, eating chips out of a bag. His brushcut hair was a throwback to the fifties. His flecked tweed jacket and narrow tie completed the image.

'Who's in charge here?' Raven demanded.

The young man came to his feet, taking a good look at his visitors.

'How did you people get up here?'

'We came up the stairs,' said Raven. Typewriters were busy in a room beyond.

The policeman braced himself. 'This is out of bounds to the public. Now if you'll just walk on down again, someone will direct you to the airport police station.'

Raven reached across the counter and grabbed the man by the lapels.

'You listen to me, you bastard! There's a murderer loose in this airport. Now get someone here to talk to me, fast!'

The young policeman picked up the phone. He was visibly shaken. He talked, continuing to look at Raven.

'I'm sorry to bother you, sir, but there's someone here who's demanding to speak to you. No, sir, a member of the public. He says there's a murderer in the airport.'

The door flew open before he could put the phone down. The newcomer was ponderously built and looked like a badly-dressed bulldog with red-rimmed eyes and sagging jowls. He raised a flap in the counter.

'Chief Superintendent Elkan. Which one of you is Raven?'

'Me,' said Raven. 'These people are with me. My wife and Paul Zeller.'

'This way,' said Elkan. They followed him through a large squad-room with a closed-circuit television system displaying different aspects of the airport on overhead screens. An ash-blonde telex operator detached herself from her machine. Elkan took the message as he went, opening a door at the far end of the room. The other three followed him into a sound-proofed room that was completely silent once he had closed the door. There were no shelves, no decorations, nothing but an ugly metal desk with three phones and a speak-box on it. The inner wall had a curtained window.

Elkan waved a beefy hand. 'Find yourselves some-where to sit. I'm not used to visitors.'

There were two chairs. Kirstie took one of them. Raven and Zeller remained standing.

'Is Mr Villiers a friend of yours?' Elkan asked Raven.

'I know who he is. I've never met him.'

'And Mr O'Callaghan?'

'He's my lawyer.'

'They're on their way here,' Elkan said heavily. He was grossly overweight and it affected his breathing. 'A police car is picking them up.'

'Then you know what this is about?' said Raven. Kirstie had crossed her ankles and was studying the green metal wall.

'Right,' said Elkan.

Raven wet his lips. 'We don't have much time.'

The suggestion appeared to anger the policeman. 'Let me worry about the time,' he said. 'I know what I'm doing. At least I *think* I know what I'm doing. It's Friday night and I'm ten officers short and somebody tells me there's a multiple killer running round in my airport. And as if that's not enough I've got an Assistant Director of Public Prosecutions on his way to see if I'm doing my job properly.'

Raven caught Kirstie's eye. She was nervous again, he could tell.

'I'm sorry,' he said. 'It couldn't be done any other way. There were reasons.'

Elkan blew hard. 'Of *course* there were reasons! What do you take me for? I know who you are and I know who Cooney is! I can hold that plane until Christmas if I want to.'

'Do that and you'll lose him,' Zeller said quietly. 'This man acts on instinct like an animal.'

Elkan swung round on him. 'What have we got here? Some kind of amateur shrink?'

'He's right,' said Raven.

Elkan blew his jowls out like a frog. 'Let me tell you people something. I give the orders on this patch. They don't come from the Director of Public Prosecutions *or* his friends!'

'I realise that,' Raven said quickly. 'But if you know who Cooney is you know everything.'

Elkan appeared to be mollified. 'He checked in twenty minutes ago so we know that he's in the airport. But we haven't been able to locate him yet. I don't want to make the arrest on the plane. There are women and children aboard.'

The telephone rang at his elbow. He jammed the receiver against his ear and passed it to Raven.

'It's for you.'

Patrick O'Callaghan came on the line. 'We should be there in half-an-hour. We've just transferred to a police car. What's going on?'

Raven cleared his throat. 'We're with the Superintendent.'

'Who's we?'

'Kirstie and Zeller.'

There was a brief pause. 'Don't talk too much until I get there.'

The line was cut off. Elkan lumbered to his feet. 'Never mind that contraption they've got downstairs. Cooney could still be armed. There are a hundred and twelve people on that plane, eighteen of them women with children.'

He pulled aside the curtain on the window, disclosing a panel of oneway glass. Only the thickness of the metal wall separated them from the Departure Hall. The benches and seats were crowded with weary travellers, some of them in transit and jet-lagged. People sprawled and gaped, surrounded by baggage and duty-free purchases. There was a high proportion of Asians and Arabs, the women slow-moving and followed by troops of bright-eyed children. It was like remembering a dream-sequence where everything moved in utter silence.

Elkan shifted his weight. 'How many people do you think are down there?'

Raven shrugged. The room they were in was higher than the Departure Hall. People were constantly coming and going.

'Hundreds,' said Elkan. 'I've got men with walkie-talkies covering every exit but we still don't have a picture of Cooney. We're waiting for one to come through on the teleprinter.'

'You don't need it.' Zeller turned from the window. 'He's over there, sitting on a bench by the souvenir shop.'

Raven spotted him immediately. Elkan wheezed to the desk and bent over the speak-box.

'What's he wearing?'

Raven replied. 'A dark-blue trenchcoat, no hat. He's sitting alone.'

Elkan relayed the information. 'Subject's wearing a dark blue trenchcoat and sitting alone near the shop. No hat. Nobody moves until I say so.'

Raven was still at the window. He saw no movement beyond the oneway glass. The men Elkan had posted were probably hidden.

Zeller turned slowly. 'Let me get this straight, Superintendent. You're worried about the other people, right?'

Elkan's small blood-shot eyes glared back balefully. 'Of course I'm bloody well worried!'

Zeller's look shared the Superintendent's concern. 'Is there any way of getting into the Departure Hall from here?' he asked.

'There's a staircase from the Squad-Room,' said Elkan. 'Why?'

'I can get Cooney out of there,' Zeller replied. There was no doubt that he meant what he said. 'Without fuss or danger to anyone. All I need is a free hand.'

The three men looked at one another. 'You're crazy,' said Raven. 'It won't work.'

'I can *make* it work,' said Zeller. He addressed himself to Elkan again. 'You don't have much time, Superintendent. Just give me a chance and have your men ready.'

Elkan's eyes retreated into pouches of flesh. The conflict in his mind showed in his face. Then, with a movement swift for a man of his bulk, he opened the door to the Squad-Room.

'You're on!' he said.

Zeller smiled as he turned to follow, a debonair figure in the loose-fitting raglan. Raven and Kirstie watched him as he crossed the Squad-Room like a man on his way to a tryst.

Elkan was back in a couple of minutes, wheezing as he took his place at the window. He seemed to be talking more to himself than to anyone else.

'He's in no danger. He'll be covered all the way. No danger.'

Zeller came into view below, making his way through the crowd, single-minded but unhurried. The door to the Squad-Room was open. A voice sounded through the speakers there.

> *British Airways announce the departure of their flight to Amsterdam. Will passengers holding boarding-cards please go to Gate Eleven.*

Raven grabbed Kirstie's hand as Cooney came to his feet below. Cooney glanced down as though making sure he had left nothing behind. Then, as he took his first step, Zeller blocked his path. The two men stood face-to-face long enough for mutual recognition. Zeller raised his hand swiftly, placing the barrel of the gun he was holding against Cooney's forehead. They saw the flash from the window, the curl of smoke that rose above the fallen body. Zeller made no attempt to escape but remained where he was, arms folded.

Panic spread like a forest fire. Figures were running in all directions, taking cover wherever they could. Elkan lurched to the talk-box.

'Get those people out of there!' he bawled. 'Clear that bloody hall!'

Zeller was out of sight by now, pinned down in the middle of plain clothes-men. Elkan rammed his hand at his sweating forehead, glaring at Raven and Kirstie. The door slammed behind him. The passengers beyond the window were still milling like ants, confused by the ring of plain clothes-men. All exits but one had been closed. There was no sign of Zeller. Raven pulled the curtain across the window and held Kirstie tight. Her body was shaking violently, her face muffled against his chest.

'It was horrible, horrible, horrible!'

She raised her tear-stained face accusingly. 'You knew that he still had that gun!'

He nodded. 'So did you,' he said gently.

Elkan's bulk filled the doorway. 'OK, your friends are here, but don't get ideas. Don't even think about leaving! You people have a lot of questions to answer.'

They could hear O'Callaghan's voice at the top of the stairs in the Squad-Room. Raven lit a cigarette and gave one to Kirstie. She took it, looking at him as if seeing him for the very first time.

'Is this how it's going to be for the rest of my life?'

'Don't worry about it,' he said quickly. 'Patrick will take care of everything.'

The lawyer was coming towards them flanked by Elkan and a man wearing a black homburg hat.

Kirstie refused to be calmed. 'I asked you a question. Is this how it's going to be for the rest of my life?'

Raven bent and kissed her mouth. 'It's going to be better,' he promised. 'I don't know how different but certainly better.'

There seemed to be nothing else he could say.

>>> If you've enjoyed this book and would like to discover more great vintage crime and thriller titles, as well as the most exciting crime and thriller authors writing today, visit: >>>

The Murder Room
Where Criminal Minds Meet

themurderroom.com

www.ingramcontent.com/pod-product-compliance
Ingram Content Group UK Ltd.
Pitfield, Milton Keynes, MK11 3LW, UK
UKHW022311280225
455674UK00004B/267